OXFORD

GW01458651

A FAMILIAR MURDER

A FAMILIAR MURDER
OXFORD MAGIC KITTEN MYSTERIES

Welcome to Oxford's Magic Kitten Shelter for Familiars!

My name's Astra. I'm single, love familiars, and am also a witch whose demon cat has more magical ability in his paw, than I have in my entire body. When I inherit my great-aunt's ramshackle mansion in the sleepy village, Witch Hollow, which nestles in Oxford's shadow, I seize the chance to break free from my family. Even if Witch Hollow is the most paranormal village in England...

Now, along with my black kitten, Satan (angel on the outside, devil on the inside), I'll show everyone that a new witch is in town.

Yet the opening event of my new business to rehome abandoned familiars ends with a witch's death. When the hot Earl Sin, a dragon shifter and my elite neighbor, turns out to be the supernatural Sheriff of Oxford, how can I prove that I'm innocent and also save my familiars?

BOOKS IN THE OXFORD SERIES

RECOMMENDED READING ORDER

ALL BOOKS ARE STANDALONE SERIES

OXFORD MAGIC KITTEN MYSTERIES

A FAMILIAR MURDER

A FAMILIAR CURSE

A FAMILIAR HEX

OXFORD PARANORMAL BOOK CLUB

BITING MR. DARCY

BOOKS IN THE REBEL SERIES

REBEL ACADEMY - WICKEDLY CHARMED
COMPLETE SERIES

CRAVE

CRUSH

CURSE

BLOOD DRAGONS

BLOOD SHACKLES

BLOOD RENEGADES

STANDALONE: BLOOD GODS

AUDIO BOOKS

LISTEN HERE...

CHAPTER ONE

Evermore Farm, Witch Hollow

ASTRA

They say *never work with kittens or demon familiars*.

At least, they *should*.

Except, I've been known as *Astra, the crazy familiar lady* for most of my life. Even for a witch that was unusual. For the last month that I've lived in Evermore Farm, which I inherited from my great-aunt, Ursula, I've woken each morning with a kitten on top of my head and a miniature unicorn warming my feet like a horned hot water bottle.

I've pretty much accepted both the *crazy* and the *familiar* part of my witch inheritance.

Who needs a man...money...*life,* when you have a farm load of abandoned familiars to help and love?

I wiped my hand across my sweating forehead, squinting into the spring morning sun. A bold flicker of black and white dived across the driveway. I watched the pair of house martins, nesting lovers, as they swooped to their round mud nest that was tucked under the eaves of the converted stables to the far side of my new property. The house martins chirped brightly.

No one liked young lovers and their PDA...or was that just me?

I pushed my hair out of my eyes. My antique cat clips were hanging down like they were making an escape attempt.

I knew how they felt.

My long blond hair tangled Rapunzel-like to my knees. My cool blue dress matched my eyes but it was marked with dirty (kitten sized) paw prints.

My demon familiar was a black kitten, Satan.

When I'd been five years old, I'd watched Satan's creation, and we'd been bonded ever since. He was loyal, loving, and possessive. He also liked to mark me as *his* witch when we had company. But then, I'd knitted him an orange witch's hat to wear today.

His scrunched-up look of horror had made it worth it.

Payback was a witch.

I traced my fingers over the paw print, before struggling to push the sign into the earth again.

Magical words swirled in flashing yellow to match the red-carpet style display of daffodils at the entrance to the farm:

Welcome to Oxford's Magic Kitten Shelter for Familiars!

Satan had asked in that sardonic way of his, whether it should truly read:

Welcome to Oxford's Home for Rebellious and Rejected Demon Familiars!

Then I'd cuddled him and hadn't wanted to let go because he had a point.

Demon familiars weren't the same as normal familiars, which were usually only granted to a witch when they turned twenty-one. Normal familiars were vampires who witches had captured and transformed.

Did I mention *normal* didn't mean boring or safe, although they were cute.

My coven, the House of Demons, created a different kind of familiar like the *designer* option: choose any animal or mythical creature, combine with a demon soul, and *voila!*

Instant demon familiar for your kid to love, amplify their magic, and collect like Pokemons.

Except, most witches wouldn't know what Pokemons were because they despised the human, non-magical world.

But I wasn't most witches.

Demons lived for centuries, aging into adulthood, even if they looked like innocent kittens or puppies for another fifty years. So, they could be passed on through generations within the covens. When a witch died (and spoiler alert, we had a high death rate), they were inherited or rejected, especially if a witch felt threatened by the familiar being more magically powerful than they were.

And no familiar should be unwanted.

I snorted. Satan had more power in his *claw*, than I had in my whole witchylicious body. Ever since I was a kid, he'd protected my secret that the only true magic I had was to connect with familiars.

Satan had spent his life doing my magical home-work for me. Plus, remembering to pay my bills, working out my accounts, and ruining non-magical movies that I hadn't seen by sneakily stealth announcing the endings.

The last one wasn't good but spin my broomstick, it was some talent.

This new business, however, was mine. I didn't need my family, the men that they kept throwing my way at *husband matchings* (and the problem with witches ignoring the non-magical world was that they missed inventions like Tinder and thought that arranged marriages were still modern), or the job in their business.

I was thirty years old this year and I was standing on my own two feet.

As long as I could just get this ever-witching sign to stand up...

I snarled, leaning all my weight on top of it.

The roots beneath the sign wiggled, pushing back defiantly.

The scent of the daffodils was sweet and intoxicating. Even the plants in the farm were enchanted and a pain in my ass. Although, I wasn't complaining about the way that the orchard and herb gardens appeared to produce whatever plants I needed no matter the season.

Ursula had always boasted about how green fingered she was and how her flowers, vegetables, fruit, and herbs would grow *evermore*.

Miss Toxic Fingers to Even Houseplants here was now in charge of a farm that looked like Sleeping Beauty's kingdom.

I mean, you try and organize a gang of ferrets, pigs, and barn owls to weed flowerbeds. Plus, the less said about my attempt to get the hamsters to hold pruning shears the better.

And don't even get me started on the mess that the minotaur, Kid, made of the lawn (but he did produce excellent manure).

Crazy Familiar Lady Rule 77: Always look for the silver lining...and the best quality manure.

"I will not lose this battle to a plant," I hissed, wriggling the sign side to side. "The House of Demons is feared across the world. Don't make me invoke Hecate or start singing."

I was bringing out the big guns.

Had I done it?

The sign began to sink into the earth.

Behind me, I could hear the low buzz of conversation and laughter at the shelter's opening event.

My new neighbors in the village of Witch Hollow, which was the most magical village in England, were gathered for the opening of my business. At least, the ones who were nosy enough to respond to the invitation that I'd had Satan send out.

I wasn't *that* crazy. I hadn't expected Satan to type with his paws. He had a spell for communicating with anyone in the world. He could hack into emails, Facebook, and even people's minds.

I did tell you demon familiar, right?

Last year, Satan and I had amused ourselves by sending tweets from important humans' accounts. Satan particularly loved pretending to be world leaders because he said that no matter how funny he made his tweets, all the non-magicals still believed them.

Satan promised that he wouldn't use that trick without me knowing, but I'd catch a glow from underneath the blankets some nights.

Satan was one devilish familiar.

This morning, I'd drilled my familiars to be on their highest cuteness level, and caterers had laid on a feast. Satan was in charge of the troops, while I put the finishing touches to the farm.

Perhaps, I'd even rehome my first familiar. But it was less Adopt a Familiar and more Adopt an Owner. The familiar had all the choice.

I'd always been certain that Satan had *chosen* me.

Did any of the witches understand that I was different to my mum, Morgan?

I shuddered. *I hoped so.*

Morgan was known less as the *crazy familiar lady* and more as the *evil laugh, whilst caging familiars for profit lady*.

Had so many villagers turned out to this event because they wanted to see for themselves whether a new wicked witch had moved into the neighborhood?

I smoothed my hands over the sign.

Perfect.

I sighed with relief, glancing over at the spires and domes of Oxford. The City was a dark blur in the distance. It was strange to be so close to the human world and yet divided and hidden.

"Good decision." I tapped my foot on the ground. "I was about to blast out a version of "Wrecking Ball" and nobody wants that."

Least of all me...

I'd sung that song too many times last summer, while sobbing and scoffing my way through industrial sized tubs of chocolate fudge ice-cream (in secret, of course). Satan had caterwauled along to accompany me. And the truly sad thing about that is he'd still sounded better than me.

What had happened last summer was another reason for this fresh start.

I'd attempted to escape from the inevitability of an arranged marriage by running away with a vampire, Starlight, only to discover that he wasn't brave enough to risk Mum's wrath.

It turned out that Morgan had discovered about our affair and had threatened to transform him into a familiar the traditional way.

Starlight had stood me up on the night that I'd waited for him to escape with me. When I'd realized that he'd abandoned me, I'd known I'd never rely on anyone but myself again.

Unless you counted Satan.

The ground rumbled and spat out the sign. I yelped, ducking.

When the sign slammed against the fence, the panel shattered. I flinched.

The fence…which my psychopathic farm had just broken…belonged to my new neighbor. On the other side of the gaping hole was a manicured mansion. I'd bet that its owners didn't have to worry about plants trying to rule them or visits from the Witch Inspectors.

Witch Hollow might be paranormal but it was also picturesque. It was ruled by the iron glove of the Witch Inspectors. If I failed to make the shelter look presentable and safe, the Inspectorate would shut us down.

I'd have failed, before I even started.

Cauldrons and broomsticks, even witches had paperwork, busybody neighbors, and petty dictators who ruled the neighborhood with rules about the length of the grass.

My brow furrowed.

How long *was* my grass? I didn't even know what color it was because Evermore Farm had rainbow grass. It changed depending on its mood.

I rested my hands on my hips. "Don't say I didn't warn you."

Channeling the chocolate fudge eating angst of last summer, I belted out Miley Cyrus' "Wrecking Ball". It didn't return the sign, but I'd learned early in my coven, never make a threat that you're not prepared to follow through on, even if the guests in the yard had stopped to watch like I was the enter-tainment.

I flushed but hey, if you commit...*commit*.

I twirled, singing my tone-deaf heart out. Then I almost fell over Satan, who was sitting where the sign had once been, low to the ground with his paws over his ears.

Everyone's a critic.

I broke off the song, and the cautious scattered applause was more embarrassing than if there'd been silence.

I was just ahead of my time.

Satan warily removed one of his paws from his ear. He was tiny even for a kitten. The knitted orange hat with gaps for his ears was almost as big as him.

Cute.

Would he wear matching mittens as well...? Because then I could do the whole rhyme about *kittens in mittens*, while dancing around the kitchen with him.

It was small moments like that in life, which truly made it worth living.

Satan's black fur sparkled like his magic was so powerful it broke through, unable to be contained.

His eyes were huge and emerald.

He could rarely mask his emotions; they were vulnerably clear in his gaze.

"*By my whiskers, is it over?*" Satan's musical, Irish voice broke into my mind telepathically. He removed his other paw, before straightening. "*I was scared you were being murdered.*"

"Oh no, my sides have split with the hilarity." I lifted my eyebrow. "Aren't you meant to be keeping an eye on Ursula's unicorn? What if he eats the wrong herbs and ends up transformed into a prince?"

Ursula's familiar was a miniature unicorn, Lucky. He was also a goth: all black with gleaming steel horn.

Why hadn't he liked it when I snuggled him and knitted him a horn warmer?

Lucky also had a weird habit of nibbling on everything. Last week, he'd eaten part of a potion for helping me to keep...regular...bowels. He'd pooped glitter for a full day and night. It'd been colorful but messy. At least I'd been able to reuse the glitter as decorations today.

Silver linings, remember?

"*Aye, that'd be a terrible fate, all right.*" Satan shuddered. "*But your murder seemed more important.*"

"You were bored, huh?"

"*You have no proof of that.*" Satan imperiously arched his back, as he wound around my ankles.

I leaned down and stroked over his head. Satan nuzzled against my hand. He never tried to hide his affection from me and in turn, I never hid my love.

"*Here's the thing of it, why don't you at least sing something decent like Black Sabbath, Metallica, or one of those lads?*" Satan demanded.

I cocked my head. "Interesting. So, it wasn't you humming along to Taylor Swift on the radio this morning?"

"*Must've been some other handsome and all-powerful black kitten.*"

"*Hmm*, must be. Just once could you pretend to obey me like a witch's familiar should?" I glanced nervously down the driveway. The Inspector was expected any minute, there was no sign up, and a new hole gaped like an accusation in the fence. "There are whole training classes on this."

Satan blinked. "*Not a chance. You never sent me on them.*"

I huffed. "That's because I knew that you were just as likely to break the instructors, as they were to break you. Plus, I'm not in favor of *breaking* anyone.*"*

"*What about...?*"

"Now is not the time for your Familiar Revenge List," I admonished. Satan flounced his tail in answer. "Today is important. How about helping it go well simply because I raised you."

Satan snickered. "*The Great Satan won't call you Mummy.*"

I blushed. "*Ehm, not what I meant.*"

This was why you don't work with kittens.

"*Anyway, I raised you,*" Satan muttered.

My expression gentled, and I scooped Satan up in my arms, before perching him on my shoulder. His claws sunk in, as he anchored himself.

He was right.

"Why'd you really come to check on me?" I asked. "You thought that I'd fallen over my feet again?"

Satan smirked. "*Possibly.*"

"Or broken something?"

Satan glanced significantly at the sign and the fence.

Whoops...

"And of course, I couldn't survive without the Great Satan."

"*It's been known.*" Satan lifted his paw, and I mirrored his actions with my hand. We'd had years to practice hiding that his magic was so much stronger than my own. Now, Satan worked with me, and so far, nobody had discovered the secret of Satan's true power. What'd happen if they ever did? "*Bad plants. On my tail, this is my witch's farm now. It's time to welcome the familiars.*"

In a blue glow, the sign spun into the air, before shooting straight into the ground with a *twang*.

And stayed there.

I held my breath, but the sign didn't move.

Satan rubbed his head against my chin. "*How about strokes for the conqueror…?*"

I grinned, stroking his ear. "You're the Grand Conqueror of Evermore."

He smelled of sweet sparkling candies. One of the wonders of being able to design familiars was that you could choose the smell. My five-year-old self had adored Love Hearts: a tiny, round candy embossed with a heart and message. With the wisdom of a kid, I'd chosen my familiar to smell of Love Hearts.

Satan could also produce Love Hearts on his tongue (Morgan's idea of an added bonus).

When I was young, Satan had delighted me by playing Hide and Seek with candies that read **I LOVE U** or **CUDDLE ME**. He still played it, but now the candies read **CATS RULE** or **FEED ME**.

Satan wiggled his tiny ass proudly. "*Your dad would be proud of you.*"

I stiffened. "Yeah, he would. But he's not here like he hasn't been for the last decade. He vanished, and I've never known why. Perhaps, now that I'm away from Mum I can find out what really happened to him. Plus, I want…"

"*If the next words out of your mouth are quiet life, then even I can't help you.*"

"I just want to prove that I can run this business by myself. No mysteries, mayhem, or…"

"*Men?*" Satan said, hopefully.

My brow darkened. "Burn me at the stake, so help me, *no men.*"

All of a sudden, a growl burst from the other side of the...broken...fence.

"We have yet to be introduced," a haughty voice, which was low and dangerous, drawled, "but already you've broken *my* fence, the rules on noise levels, and my ears with your singing. Is it not enough that I have to live next to your monstrosity of a property? Yet now you've also opened some sort of camp for rebel familiars."

Satan preened.

I stared at my next-door neighbor, who was leaning in the space where the fence had once been with his arms crossed over his muscular chest.

Wow, he was tall.

His midnight tumble of hair fell over high cheek-bones. His black trousers and jacket, which were embroidered with silver orchids, were cut like he was in the military.

Should I be saluting?

He definitely made me feel like I was on parade. I rubbed ineffectually at the paw prints on my dress, and his eyes narrowed.

Okay, was he about to bark at me for the state of my uniform and demand that I *drop and give him twenty?*

I slouched, crossing my arms in turn. I wasn't soldier material but I wouldn't be intimidated on my own land either.

Did that make me the rebel?

I eyed my neighbor back.

So, this was the reclusive owner of the pristine mansion next door, who I'd never seen before...? I'd begun to think that he was a ghost (which in this village was possible).

At least he wasn't a vampire.

His eyes, which were as pale as silver and glimmered in the light, met mine with an intent gaze.

There was no way that I'd let him see the way I shivered.

Mysteries, mayhem, and men were all burning at the stake bad, remember?

Look, I could already feel their warmth licking through me, as he stepped through the shattered remains of the fence. He stormed towards me in a hot (*bad, bad, very bad*) whirlwind of outraged neighbor.

But then, his magic fluttered out of him like decadent silver bat wings, as his eyes flamed.

It was beautiful.

My breath caught.

He was a dragon shifter.

A *silver* dragon shifter, which was the fiercest kind.

In Hecate's name, what did I do to deserve this (apart from everything he'd accused me of, but never let the truth get in the way of a good lamentation)?

The Witch Inspector would be here any minute to either approve or close my business, and my uptight next-door neighbor was a dragon shifter, who looked ready to burn down my business.

CHAPTER TWO

Evermore Farm, Witch Hollow

ASTRA

The handsome shifter with molten silver eyes vibrated on the edge of bursting into his dragon form and burning down Evermore Farm. He smartly clasped his hands behind his back like he was restraining himself. His magic coiled out of him, however, in fluttering silver streaks towards me.

It was spellbinding.

I still took a step back because Starlight, who'd abandoned me, had been equally gorgeous and mesmerizing.

Yet he'd also been deadly underneath it like a tiger…*or a dragon*. Both could rip out your heart, use it as a chew toy, and spit it out in a bloody puddle. *Then* make you embarrassingly howl out "Wrecking Ball."

I shuddered. I couldn't live through that again and I knew that Satan wouldn't survive it.

The shifter's magic licked across my cheek like it couldn't resist the temptation (Satan had invented a special potion to make my skin silky soft), dragging at the magic deep inside me and entwining with it.

Okay, that was *way* too intimate.

What'd happened to magical personal space?

Satan hissed, subtly winding his magic around me, at the same time as stinging the shifter's.

Satan's magic cocooned me in the ultimate cock block.

Having a demanding cat alone was perfect for that.

The shifter grimaced and withdrew his magic with a shrug of his shoulders, although he eyed me with a wary respect like the power that he'd sensed had been *mine*.

That was right, Alpha jerk dragon: fear the scary all-powerful witch.

Satan shot the shifter a smug look from his place perched on my shoulder.

"My apologies," the shifter said, grudgingly, "dragon instincts, you know?"

I turned on my heel. I needed to get back to the opening, before the Witch Inspector turned up.

"Don't let those instincts hit you on your dragon ass on the way out," I called over my shoulder.

"Wait," he called with an edge of desperation that surprised me. I hesitated. Psycho dragons were not on my To Do List today. I sighed, before turning back to him. "I suppose my invitation was lost in the post…?"

He strained to look past me at the buzz of other villagers in front of my cottage.

The yard was so crowded that the familiars had to scurry between legs, swoop in the skies, or hop on the guests' startled shoulders. It looked like almost the entire village had turned out.

Why did the shifter care that he hadn't been invited? Wasn't he the recluse, whose sole reason to march over here was to complain?

But if that was true, why was he trying to hide crushing disappointment mixed with wary hope beneath that haughty mask of his?

Crack my broomstick, was he hoping that I'd invite him to join us?

And if so, he had the worst manners that I'd come across and I worked with demon familiars.

Of course, he *should've* received an invite.

I raised an eyebrow at Satan, who instantly plastered on his innocent face.

The problem with having a magical familiar like

Satan was that he always knew more than me (and I was witch enough to admit that), and he was always scheming.

On the other hand, it was his most adorable feature.

Satan looked the dragon shifter up and down. *"You're old and posh. It's like this, see, you probably don't even have a computer. I bet you only have antiques and stuff. So, how could you receive the email for this event?"*

The shifter flushed, flustered. "I admit that I possess a quantity of antiques, however, I also own a computer. On the other hand, I'm not old...I mean, not in dragon years... I'm the younger son; it's my brother who's the Duke. I'm merely the Earl..." *A witching earl was my next-door neighbor?* Then his mouth snapped shut, and his eyes narrowed at Satan. "How can I hear that kitten?"

He spat out *kitten* like it meant *snake*. Except, some of my favorite familiars were snakes. Perhaps, I should've said *dung beetle*.

So, not a cat lover then.

Satan's fur fluffed up in outrage, at the same time as my own hackles rose.

Sweet Hecate, if a man didn't love cats then he was dead inside.

Starlight had adored Satan, and he'd been a vampire. Except, the truth was that vampires were

Fallen Angels, so Satan had taken full advantage of sleeping on Starlight's wings, treating them like movable feathery beds.

To be honest, I think it was the only reason that Satan had wanted me to bond with Starlight.

I stroked Satan's head. "You can hear Satan because he *wants* you to. Some witches don't grant their familiars that freedom, but let's just say that Satan can choose who he talks to, where he goes, and what time he wakes me up in the mornings." Satan snickered. "That last one is up for negotiation though if it's abused."

Wow, did Satan abuse it.

Exhibit A, this morning: *Rise and shine, my witch. It's 3 a.m. and my stomach's awake and demanding tuna.*

The shifter blinked. "You let him tell people lies…?"

Satan winked. "*And insult them.*"

"Sounds right," I agreed. "But as I told you, there's no *let* about it. Since we're total strangers here, I'll explain that I'm Astra of the House of Demons, but even though my mum's notorious for controlling demon familiars, I'm more for…"

"*Being controlled by them?*" Satan purred.

"Unhelpful," I whispered.

"You and the cat parrot on your shoulder are strange." The shifter cocked his head, and dark hair tumbled across his eyes like he was trying to work me out.

Good luck on that.

It was more fun playing with this earl dragon than I'd expected.

Morgan had never thought that I'd break away from the family business, and no one amongst the covens had guessed that a witch of the House of Demons would choose to work with the rejects of the familiar world.

Doing the unexpected was working for me so far.

I smiled sweetly, enjoying the flash of confusion on my neighbor's face. "Why don't you join us? We have these delicious cocktails that are enchanted to taste like your choice of flavor on each sip, and the village caterers have laid on a feast." My eyes lit up. "You may even find a familiar you'd like to rehome." At the shifter's horrified expression, Satan chuckled. "A panther, perhaps," I muttered.

"What was that?" The shifter demanded.

"Nothing."

The shifter *harrumphed*, before leaping over the remains of the fence and okay, that was impressive.

In no way was I noticing his bunched muscles or athletic legs.

Of course not.

"*Lay off, I'm the mini-panther around here,*" Satan complained.

I rolled my eyes. "Obviously."

"*Don't patronize the Great Satan but do stroke him.*"

I lifted Satan off my shoulder and cradled him in my arms, so that I could get in a full-on belly stroke.

The shifter raised an elegant eyebrow. "He has you well trained, Astra."

Satan purred. "*Aye, it took years of hard work, but the results speak for themselves.*"

When I dumped Satan in a ball of disgruntled fluff amongst the daffodils, it was the shifter's turn to laugh.

I was shocked at how musical his laugh was. I could get used to that.

But well trained my witchy ass…

When the shifter marched closer, his spicy scent of myrrh wound around me, wrapping me in its warmth. "Who am I to turn down such hospitality? Wait, I know…" He held out his hand. "I'm Earl Sinclair, at your service. Although, my friends call me Sin because…" His smile was dangerous. "…Perhaps, it's more fun if you discover that for yourself."

"Goodie, games. My favorite." *Unintentional innuendo alert.* Why were his eyes darkening like that? Time for desperate backpedaling. "You know, like non-sinful online gaming, Cluedo, or poker. Don't try and beat me at card games because this face has no tells."

"*Uh-huh.*" Sin's butterfly long black lashes were criminally unfair. Men shouldn't be allowed to have lashes like that without mascara. "I'm reading you just fine right now."

Mr Boastful Dragon.

When his hand rested on the hilt of a curved scabbard, which was strapped to his side, my eyes widened. "You brought a weapon over to complain about the noise? *Oh no, my new terrifying witch neighbor and her shelter for wild familiars, I'd better strap on my sword.*"

He blinked. "Was that meant to be an impression of me? I most certainly do not sound like a cowardly prince with a stick up my behind. I need my sword…"

"You have a sword fetish?"

His jaw clenched. "It's ceremonial. At least, for me. Dragons from my Court…warriors from it…fight with these, but I don't any longer."

"And is that a ceremonial gun in your pocket, or are you just pleased to see me?"

Sin looked trapped. "I don't have a gun."

I blushed at the same time as him. *Don't look down at his crotch.*

Stupid innuendo mouth…

Satan glanced between Sin and me, before deliberately breaking the tension. "*Satan and Sin sounds like a fine duo.*" Satan preened. "*Like a crime fighting team.*

Help, the world's in peril because of the evil chickens." Satan was caught up in a war with the chickens (entirely normal, non-magical ones that I kept for their eggs). Last week, he'd tried to make friends with them, expecting them to talk back but instead, they'd chased him. One of the few rules I had was that he mustn't use magic against non-magical animals. "*Who shall we call?*"

"Ghostbusters?" I hazarded.

Satan puffed out his chest. "*Satan and Sin, that's who. You do want to be saved from the terrorist chickens, right?*"

"Why not Sin and Satan?" Sin drawled. "After all, *I'm* the earl."

Satan waved his tail at him in his version of a rude gesture.

But the fact that he was Earl Sinclair *was* a problem.

Witches had a complex relationship with dragon bluebloods. Being aristocracy meant that they were the leaders of their people or in positions of power.

Sin's magic must be powerful.

Covens either fought, screwed, or had an uneasy truce with shifters. I should keep up with that sort of thing but Mum had always moaned that with me, if something wasn't about familiars or books, it went in one ear and then out the other.

Nothing had changed.

To be honest, I was regretting that now. Were witches at war with dragons still?

As I now was living next to one, I was hoping *not*.

Witch Hollow was the only village in England, however, where all supernatural races were supposed to put aside their differences, wars, and past grudges to live together. My great-aunt had chosen it for that reason. She'd rejected my family as firmly as I was.

I'd admired her for fighting against witch prejudice and her desire to live without hurting other races.

For her desire for freedom.

The goal of Witch Hollow was for peace and harmony. But was that even possible? After all, they appeared to be ruled by Counselors, a Mayor, and the Witch Inspectors.

My lip curled at the thought, and I snarled.

Wait, I didn't just snarl out loud…? That was the downside of living with familiars.

Goth unicorns who sprayed your bed with glitter, rarely spoke more than a grunted word, and loved sleeping, didn't encourage good social interaction.

I'd always imagined that it'd be like living with human college students.

I reddened.

Sin blinked. "Ah, now I understand about the panther."

"What…?"

Satan sat up. "*This massive silver dragon is growing on me. He can stay.*"

"I'm glad that I have your blessing," I deadpanned.

"*You're welcome.*"

Sin smiled, brightly. He gestured towards my cottage. "Shall we?"

I nodded.

But then, an ancient witch with her hair pulled back into a severe bun and wire glasses balanced on the tip of her sharp nose, tottered down the driveway towards me, clutching a clipboard.

The Witch Inspector.

"*Look at her there with her clipboard and files.*" Satan hissed. "*The banality of evil.*"

Sin attempted to smother his laugh in his palm.

I stiffened, pushing my hair back from my face and straightening the cat clips.

This was it.

My business either passed or was closed on the first day of my new life.

Please Hecate, protect my familiars.

A puppy Pomeranian demon familiar trotted at her side like a teddy bear. The familiar's fur was orange like a fox. The puppy was so tiny (it could've fitted on the palm of my hand) that it struggled to keep up, falling over its paws.

The witch patted her thigh impatiently.

"Hurry up, Precious," the Inspector snapped. "If you make me late, you'll wait at home in the cage next time."

I winced both at her sharp tone to her familiar and at the *Precious*.

What cruel and unusual punishment to name a familiar *Precious*. But then, I'd designed mine to smell like candy.

Who was I to cast stones?

Sin crossed his arms and to my surprise, stepped in front of me like he was protecting me from the Inspector. "You're a beacon of mercy and kindness as always, Lanira."

"That's Inspector Marchbanks to you, Sin," the Inspector, Marchbanks, sniffed.

Marchbanks looked Sin up and down dismissively.

"And that's Earl Sinclair to you," Sin gritted out.

His eyes flashed, and his magic spun out in wings.

Was Marchbanks deliberately baiting him?

Precious panted and collapsed in a ball of fluff at her side amongst the daffodils. Satan narrowed his eyes at him, and Precious cocked his head.

Any moment there'd be a fluffy cat and dog battle.

Brilliant.

Marchbanks' smile was sly. "Burned down any houses recently, *Earl* Sinclair?"

Now there was some serious dragon prejudice.

I hissed in a shocked breath. "Not all dragons are pyromaniacs…"

I trailed off, as Sin twisted to me, making desperate *hushing* gestures.

Marchbanks' smile widened. "I'd heard that you held modern beliefs. Well, you've drawn the short straw then because you've moved next to one who's infamous for it."

Infamous…?

Witching heavens, couldn't he at least be *famous* for it?

Sin's broad shoulders slumped like a chastened school kid.

Marchbanks peered at Sin over her glasses. "Let me rephrase it: are you here now intending to burn down this property?"

My cheeks flamed at the injustice of her demanding that of one of my guests. I opened my mouth to insist that she stop harassing Sin, when Sin answered by tilting his hand with the gesture meaning *fifty-fifty*.

Typical.

My righteous indignation deflated, and I huffed. "Actual property owner over here."

When Marchbanks stepped around Sin and fixed me with a beady stare, I regretted drawing her attention.

What'd happened to my survival instincts?

Satan had told me that I was always one to tempt fate: dabbing perfume on my neck to tempt vampire nuzzling next to my jugular or putting my profile on Tinder for dates with humans.

How was I to know that those who included a Snapchat handle (and raised in a coven, until my personal social media kitten, Satan, explained it to me, I thought Snapchat must be something to do with crocodiles), were likely to want to exchange naked photos?

Humans had weird obsessions with photographing private parts of their bodies…and not even the pretty bits, if you ask me.

I'd never risk dating non-magical men again. They plotted more than Satan. Except, it appeared to be more plotting to get into my pants.

Marchbanks clutched her clipboard tighter. "Well, Astra of the House of Demons, I'd say that it was my honor to welcome you to our village, but that would be a lie." I gaped at her. *Kudos for the brutal honesty.* "We're a beautiful and renowned village with every-thing in its place, and everyone *knowing* their place. Why would we need faulty, broken, and outcast famil-iars here? It goes against all witch order for a familiar to possess more magic than their owner, and that's what your demons risk...unicorn, griffin, and mino-taur... They don't deserve a home."

"Fair and impartial as always," Sin muttered.

Was it frowned upon to hex your Inspector?

"Let's agree to disagree," I forced myself to say, while balancing on one leg and using my other ankle to hold Satan back from launching himself at Marchbanks.

"*Let me at her*," Satan hissed, struggling against my ankle. "*I'll show her that my claws deserve a home in her arse.*"

This time, Sin couldn't hide his laugh.

Marchbanks' eyes narrowed. "Already the premises aren't secure." She pointed her bony finger at the broken fence. My heart clenched. Frogs and toads, if I only had more magical power, then I wouldn't have fought to control the farm and ended up smashing the fence. I'd battled my whole life to survive in a magical world with only Satan to help me. *Don't let this be the day that it defeated me.* "I'll have to fail this Shelter for Magical Familiars, if you can't even be responsible enough to secure its boundaries."

My eyes smarted with tears, and Sin caught my gaze.

His expression softened. Then he turned to Marchbanks.

"I broke the fence," Sin lied, smoothly enough to be disconcerting. He bent his biceps in a display that curled warmth through me, before kissing them, and Marchbanks grimaced. Satan snickered, and to my surprise, so did the Pomeranian. "You know, with all my brutish out of control dragony strength."

Why was Sin helping me?

He hadn't wanted to live next to a *monstrosity of a property* or a *rebel camp for familiars* before. What had Marchbanks done that he hated her enough to protect me from her?

"*Beast*," Marchbanks snarled. "You should be collared."

Okay, well that explained it.

Sin paled. "How interesting. Thank you for your opinion. Be sure to bring it up again with the Counselors or how about another petition? It was most *exciting* last time not knowing whether my freedom was going to be stolen from me."

Furious, Marchbanks stamped towards my sign. Her *stompy* feet, with weirdly large shoes that looked too large for her, crushed my daffodils that squeaked in protest.

Then she tapped the top of my sign. "This is smart."

I relaxed. *Thank Hecate.*

"But it's an inch too high." Marchbanks wrote something down on her clipboard.

I froze. "Come on, seriously?"

Marchbanks waved her hand over the paperwork, and a black mark was stamped.

I peered at it in shock. "Did you just add a sad face emoji?"

She gave a cruel twist of a smile. "Don't worry, I have a feeling that it'll soon be joined by many friends."

Satan waved his clawed paw through the air. *"Her arse is mine. Nobody misuses the power of an emoji."*

For once, I was glad that Satan wasn't allowing her to hear him.

Marchbanks shot me a final censorious look, before bustling past me and down the driveway towards the opening with her fluffy puppy bouncing after her.

I didn't expect the way that Sin smiled at me reassuringly, before he followed her.

I took a deep breath, and my pulse pounded. I already had one sad face emoji, and I doubted that he'd be lonely for long.

This shelter was *everything* to my familiars, Satan, and me.

What would happen to us if Marchbanks killed it?

CHAPTER THREE

Evermore Farm, Witch Hollow

SATAN

I, the Great Satan, shall share with you the special secrets and stories of the demon familiars.

You're welcome.

Just close your eyes and repeat *Kitten Satan, Kitten Satan, Kitten Satan* three times in front of a mirror.

Bet I made you do it, didn't I? My witch fell for it too.

And all it'll cost you is your eternal Soul.

Whoops, sometimes that just slips out, see, force of habit.

It's like this, all it'll really cost you is the promise of eternal strokes.

Deal...?

I ducked underneath the table in the farm's yard that groaned underneath the weight of cakes, sandwiches, and pies. I wrinkled my nose, sniffing the delicious scents of mingling foods.

I tilted my head, listing the fillings, since I was the Cat Detective when it came to working out the leftovers that'd be ending up on my own plate.

On my whiskers, salmon, turkey, beef slices…*and cheese*.

Brilliant!

I bounced up and down with excitement, before freezing with embarrassment. I pretended that I was only washing an awkward spot behind my ear. Nobody knew that trick, all right? Then I pushed against the knitted orange hat and was glad that cats couldn't blush.

I was only wearing the orange outrage to my dignity to make my witch happy.

I'd do anything for her, even wear silly hats.

As soon as this event was over, I'd hide behind a bush and chew a hole through the hat. My witch would believe that I was attacked by a passing magpie, who'd wanted to add it to his nest of *treasures*.

That was how you sneaked in a compliment, even in a dastardly plot.

What a shame that I wouldn't be able to wear the hat again...

So, here's the thing about the humiliating bouncing: I *might* have this mild (*serious*) cheese obsession.

Cheese was created to tempt us into sin.

Being a familiar is to have no control over your life. But my witch, Astra, has never acted like the other witches. She let me choose what I did and to decide to learn magic alongside her.

What am I saying? *I rule her...but that's our little secret.*

My witch simply doesn't admit it, unless I threaten to claw her favorite dress (the hideous lace one that she loved because the vampire with the snuggly wings said she looked like a *Queen of the Night* in it).

So, to prove that I was free, despite what the covens believe about familiars, I set myself Satan Personal Achievement Awards to unlock.

You can bet my kitteny arse that stealing cheese was one such award.

Every cat must have ambitions.

One of my proudest moments was when my witch had just turned six, and I'd managed to slink into the kitchen and sink my teeth into a whole block of cheese.

Satan Personal Achievement Unlocked.

I'd dragged the cheese halfway up the stairs to my witch's room, before her ma had discovered me.

I shuddered. Now *there* was a wicked witch who had a broomstick stuck in a place, where nothing was meant to be inserted.

Perhaps, the karma that she'd earned for forcing us demons into fluffy pets shoved it in there?

Never piss off the Karma Fairy: he was huge, hairy, and had a wicked sense of humor.

I peered through the legs of the guests. The cottage behind the yard was ancient and a ramshackle burst of lemon yellow and timber beams. The owls had spent the night decorating it with banners:

Welcome to Oxford's Magic Kitten Shelter for Familiars!

My fur bristled.

I'd never been around so many different paranormals at the same time: vampires, shifters, reapers, fae, and witches. The smells, noise, and magic of so many at once was overwhelming.

The Great Satan did not cower.

I whimpered, backing away and shaking my head. My own magic caressed around me, attempting to keep out the vibrating wrongness of the conflicting magic.

If I could only block it out without transporting them all to the moon... *That wasn't an option, right?*

I shook my head. My witch wouldn't like it. So, something less drastic.

Music from Rage Against the Machine, Linkin Park, or one of those lads was loud enough to drown out anything.

My lip curled. *Taylor Swift, my tail.*

Was it my fault that her songs were so devilishly catchy?

I wove a Music Spell around the cottage, and Bullet for the Valentine's "Waking the Demon" exploded out like a punch.

The guests jumped, spilling their cocktails. The familiars who'd been working as servers headbanged or jumped up and down wildly. My witch shot me a fondly exasperated glance.

Away with you, I didn't imagine the fondly.

She was chatting to that giant of a dragon shifter, Sin. I narrowed my eyes at the cat hater. *Just let him try something.* He might have wings and fire, but he also wore a suit with flowers all over it.

He was marked down as my next scratching post.

Now, where was the Inspector?

Marchbanks could destroy everything that I'd built (with a wee bit of help from my witch), for my pals. What if it meant that the other familiars were stolen from us and given to cruel owners who didn't allow them to sleep on beds, set up false social media accounts, and plan world domination? You know, all the basic familiar rights?

When I twisted to the side, however, I bumped into a ball of fluff.

"*Oww*," I yowled, falling onto my arse. "*We've been invaded by Tribbles*."

The familiar silently studied me. He looked like a cartoon come to life. *Hmm, was that possible?* I'd add it to my Satan's Plots List.

I sighed, meeting the Inspector's puppy, Precious', dark-eyed gaze with a glare of my own. "*I've promised my witch best behavior. Fair play to you for trying to take me on because you're the only dog I've ever met, who's as tiny as I am, but if you want to fight, then name the time and place. Just not until after the inspection*."

Precious cocked his head.

No answer.

Well, dogs were idiots.

"*What are you looking at?*" I hissed.

A sparkling sweet Love Heart popped onto my tongue, and I spat it out.

I WILL SCRATCH U

Precious only wagged his tail. "*Hail Satan!*"

I gaped at him.

Precious' voice was regal and Scottish. He was probably older than me. Us demons aged slowly and the poor puppy had probably been with the Inspector for decades.

Had it turned him crazy?

Still, I preened. "*Cheers for the over-the-top but satanically correct greeting. Next time try the official Latin: Ave Satana. But keep it down because we don't want to set off all the other familiars.*" I glanced at my witch. I didn't think she'd rate *best behavior* as coaching the Inspector's puppy as my new follower. *Could I help my natural charisma?* I gave a sly grin. "*Or why not try setting it to music like a Gregorian chant but without the heavenly nonsense?*"

The humans' Satan memes were bad enough. But then, I had invented some Elmo ones because I'd always wanted a Muppet to worship a demon.

Precious leveled me with another assessing gaze.

Then he barked, "*Hail Satan! Hail Satan! Hail Satan! Hail Satan! Hail...*"

I pounced on Precious, tumbling him to the floor. Panting, I stared down at him, but he only licked my face.

Yuck.

I rubbed my face against his belly to wipe myself dry, but he only wriggled happily like I was giving him a belly rub.

When I glanced up, my witch was shooting me a disapproving look and this time, there was no fond-ness in the mix.

Damn my whiskers.

Sin pointed at me like I was the dictator who'd threatened to take over the Court of the Silver Dragons (and don't think that I hadn't considered it). "This is why I don't want a familiar. You won't convince me."

My witch wrapped her hand around his bicep (I never trusted anyone with biceps that large) in a way that I didn't like. "I'm sorry. Are you allergic to fur? Were you traumatized by a bat? Insulted by a beaver or...?"

"It was my ex." Sin shifted uncomfortably.

My witch grimaced. "She was a beaver?"

Sin chuckled. "More like a spider, but that'd be an insult to arachnids. She owned a cat…Ninja…who hated me. I only had to enter the house, and he'd launch an attack."

What did Sin expect? The cat *was* trained in martial arts.

My witch gasped. "Why? What had you done to her?"

"Nothing." Sin took a sip of his cocktail and then licked his lips appreciatively. "My wings, whiskey and chocolate together. This drink is weirdly delicious." He sighed. "Ninja's mistress spoiled her. She received so much attention that she refused to share it with me."

Well, wasn't he a Bitter Dragon?

Even a familiar could listen...eavesdrop...on their witch, and who they chose as their mate was the most important decision in their life.

If a witch went along with an arranged marriage to a son from another coven, then their kids would be mortal. Here's the thing, that meant at some point, I'd be inherited or *unwanted.*

Whereas, if my witch married a dragon shifter who lived for centuries, her kids would live as long as me.

It had possibilities.

I'd been keen on the vampire for the same reason, but I didn't blame him for not having the balls to face my witch's ma. Who'd take the risk of being turned into a familiar and losing your freedom?

Only someone who was truly in love.

My witch was better off without Starlight. She deserved someone who'd risk everything for her.

Who'd die or kill for her...like me.

I didn't understand all the weird dating rites, but I understood love.

I'd help find the right mate for my witch.

The only problem was that this dragon shifter and my witch appeared to be opposites. They liked each other less than I liked bones in my fish, didn't they?

Precious squirmed underneath me, and absent-mindedly I kneaded his fur with my paws. He whined happily.

Then I realized what I was doing and scrabbled away from him. He grinned at me like *he* was the king who'd tricked me into serving him.

No one turned Satan into a servant.

"*Now just hold on, laddy.*" Precious bounced towards me. "*I was about to hire you as my new Play Slave.*" *I knew it.* "*Sorry,* servant. *My last one never liked it when I mixed those two up.*"

I stiffened. "*What happened to your last Play Servant?*"

When you just know that you shouldn't ask the question, but your traitorous mouth won't listen to you...

All of a sudden, Precious' large eyes brimmed with tears, and he whimpered.

Was it part of my duties to comfort upset puppies?

"*There, there.*" I awkwardly patted his shoulder with my paw. "*Imagine that you're telling a priest, only I'm a kitten, more demonic and with...*" I caught myself, remembering the knitted hat, "*...the same interesting dress sense.*"

Precious sniffed. "*My Mistress sold him because his magic became too powerful. You need to watch yourself, because she doesn't believe that familiars should be more magical than their witch.*"

I winced, wrapping my magic more tightly around myself. "*I've no idea what you're talking about, puppy.*"

He nudged me with his nose, as if in apology. "*Hail Satan!*"

I snickered. "*That's better.*"

"*She intends to fail the shelter,*" Precious whispered.

My eyes widened, and I looked around for Marchbanks

After all the effort that the other familiars, my witch, and I had put into taming Evermore Farm and putting on this event, the Witch Inspector had always been planning to shut us down.

My poor, poor, witch.

Meeooww...

My witch stared at me in shock.

Suddenly, I wished that she'd scoop me up and cradle me in her arms. I'd never tell her how much I loved that, and her comforting lavender scent.

I frantically looked around for Marchbanks, who was swimming like a shark between the guests, tapping the cottage's door, posts that led to the fields, and the floor, nibbling on a cupcake, and then marking those damned sad face emojis on her clipboard.

The Great Satan must free the emojis from the hands of their oppressor.

Furious, I glowed sapphire blue.

Nobody threatened those who I loved. How would she like it if I stamped a sad face emoji where her sour face now was?

It'd suit Marchbanks: her true character shown on the outside.

The Karma Fairy would be proud of my work.

I smirked, but then Precious leaped on me, tumbling me around in a hissing ball of fluff. "*Nay, Play Servant, don't. This is what she wants. Then she can brand the familiars dangerous and take away all of you, like she sold my pal.*"

Precious and I banged into the corner of the food table. Instantly, we stopped fighting and together stared up at the wobbling table.

Uh-oh...

In a crash that made me wince, the carefully stacked plates of cakes and sandwiches tumbled onto our heads.

The guests jumped back from the chaos. Cream and turkey slices splattered over my head.

That was my new hat done for. *What a shame.*

Precious and I stared at each other, before we burst into laughter. Then we dived on the food because once food hit the floor for longer than three seconds, it transformed into leftovers.

That was a well-known familiar rule, right?

Precious chomped on a pork pie, and I hit the motherload. A cheese sandwich!

Come to my belly, you fine specimen of cheese deliciousness...

But just as I was about to Unlock yet another

Personal Achievement Award, Marchbanks marched towards Precious and me with a glare that could've frozen us to stone.

"What did I tell you? I warned that you must act like the familiar trainers have taught you. Now you'll stay in your cage, until I can be certain that you won't shame me," Marchbanks snarled. Precious whined, hiding his head under his paws. My eyes narrowed. That was what *she* thought, but Precious felt like mine now, and *mine* didn't get caged. "This is why familiars need a firm hand. He spends less than an hour with *your* demon and he's become a delinquent."

Delinquent. How kind of her. But no crimes had ever been *proved.*

A criminal is someone who's bad at their job because they got caught.

I'm good at my job.

My witch clenched her fists. All the guests had stopped to watch the drama.

"Perhaps," my witch gritted out, "it was *your* puppy's bad influence on *my* kitten."

I chuckled.

Yeah, right.

Then I sobered at the look that my witch shot me and attempted to look sweet, instead.

"Nonsense." Marchbanks became red with rage. Actually, I'd never seen anyone such a crimson shade and on each word, she turned startlingly redder. Even my witch hadn't become that angry when I'd borrowed her expensive shampoo to make my fur all poofy. A kitten has to look his best. Precious barked in alarm. "Precious is acting out, your kitten is the devil incarnate, and there are so many infractions that there's no longer any unmarked paper left." *On my whiskers, she was going to close us down.* My magic whipped through me in distress. "It's my great pleasure to fai..."

All of a sudden, Marchbanks' eyes widened, and she choked.

Her red cheeks turned to curling flames. She raised her smoking hands in front of herself in shock, dropping the clipboard, as her fingers flared like candles.

Then before she could say one more poisonous word, she self-combusted with a bang that sent the guests ducking for cover, leaving behind nothing but a pile of ash in her oversized boots.

That was a fine sight.

My belief in the Khama Fairy was totally vindicated.

Precious howled mournfully.

Instantly, in the middle of the feast of leftovers, I cuddled Precious because puppy be damned, it wasn't often that you saw your own witch burn alive in a fit of rage.

That was what'd happened, right…?

Apart from Precious, however, nobody appeared upset that they'd witnessed Marchbanks' death, even though they were her neighbors from the village. There was shock but no crying into handkerchiefs or wails of *why, she was the best of us* breast beating.

Except, why was everyone turning to glance in horror at *me* now?

Why were they pointing at my witch?

Marchbanks had been just about to close down the shelter. She'd died a magically violent death with the words that would've destroyed us on her lips.

Well, that'd do it.

Brilliant.

Sin's expression was grim. "Stay where you are. Don't touch the ashes. I'll need to talk to each of you."

Why was he avoiding my witch's gaze?

"Bossy." My witch blanched, and she shook. She poked Sin in the side. "This happens to be my property and my...exploding Inspector. If you want to make yourself useful, spread those pretty wings of yours and go fly to fetch whoever's in charge of figuring out why a witch would act like a cigarette."

Sin's jaw clenched. "My *pretty* wings don't need to take me anywhere. *I'm* the Sheriff of Oxford, and this is *my* murder inquiry."

My witch swallowed. "Can I take back the *bossy* comment?"

Sin arched his brow. "You can be interviewed first, along with your familiars."

My witch nodded.

When I caught her worried gaze, I meowed, innocently.

I'd always hated the story of the *Boy Who Cried Wolf*.

My witch and I had only just moved to the village, and now we were suspected of being murderers.

CHAPTER FOUR

Evermore Farm, Witch Hollow

SATAN

The timing and method of Marchbanks' killing was a wee bit suspicious. See, I'd make a Great Cat Detective, as well as the Great Satan.

Mostly, I deduced that the criminal was an *idiot*.

Marchbanks was killed in front of at least half the village as witnesses *and* the Sheriff of Oxford.

Yet the criminal had a good chance of getting away with it because lucky for them, the Sheriff was even more of an idiot. He thought that my witch and I were the chief suspects simply because we had motive, means, and opportunity.

Pfft, technicalities.

You'll never take me alive…

Before I could make my escape from underneath the food table (because using my magic to disappear wouldn't be a good way of proving how harmless I was), my witch darted to block me. Then she ducked down, soothing her magic over me, which had the side effect of freezing me in place.

It was almost like she knew me.

Her magic when it came to familiars was powerful.

Precious whined, and his tail dropped between his legs like he expected my witch to hurl insults at me or spank my kitteny arse.

It was lucky that Marchbanks had already self-combusted or for traumatizing Precious, I'd have cursed her to get a paper cut every time that she'd touched one of her damn files.

Death by a Thousand Paper cuts might take longer than the normal style of execution, but I was a patient cat.

My witch graced Precious with a stroke that should've been *mine*, before pulling me close and whispering, "I know that I've already broken my promise of no mysteries or mayhem."

At once, her power over me became no more than caressing waves, and I could move again.

I licked a blob of cream off my nose, before glancing significantly at Sin. "*Or men.*"

My witch grimaced at the state of my hat, before carefully taking it off.

Score.

"Don't worry, I'll knit you another one," she promised.

"*No rush.*"

She stood, cradling me to her chest. I snuggled into her floral scent, which smelled of safety, home, and love.

The other guests milled around the yard in shocked silence, although it didn't appear to stop them sipping their cocktails. The demon familiars huddled against the wall of the cottage, where Sin had ordered them, like a line-up.

My witch narrowed her eyes at Sin, who was poking at Marchbanks' ash filled shoes.

What did Sin expect to find in them: Marchbanks' dentures?

"I know that I swore I'd be burned at the stake if I chose the *men* option," my witch shuddered, "but having just been shown a lovely snapshot of that, *I take it back.*"

I kneaded her with my paws for comfort. "*Fair on you. But how screwed are we?*"

My witch sighed. "I'll protect you and all the familiars."

"*That screwed then.*"

My witch lifted me onto her shoulder. "Okay, we'll protect each other."

I nodded, proudly. "*Better.*"

I stared at the dragon shifter, who'd straightened now and was studying me with a speculative gaze.

Why wouldn't he wish to look on my gorgeous black kittenness?

I puffed out my chest. "*A cat may look at a dragon...and prove that he didn't kill any familiar caging, emoji abusing Inspector, who probably deserved to—*"

My witch slammed her palm over my mouth like I wasn't talking to her telepathically; it must be tough for her to keep up with a cat of my magical ability. "Sin can still hear you, huh?"

I grinned wickedly. "*Possibly.*"

When I licked her palm, she pulled it away. "What are you plotting?"

I gasped. "*Lay off, why do you always assume that I...?*" I snickered. I couldn't even keep up the false moral outrage. "*Would you take it easy? Earl About to Charge Us with Murder thinks that you have enough magical mojo to pull off the curse, poisoning, hex, or whatever burned up Marchbanks. You can't even magically order your playlists. Don't you think we have to show Sin?*"

"My playlists?"

I rolled my eyes. "*Perhaps later. First, that you barely have magic.*"

Sin's gaze shot to mine, and his brow arched.

My witch flushed. "But that's secret."

"*Aye, and secrets aren't much good if you're sent to supernatural jail or worse, the Rebel Academy, as punishment, unless you trade them for chocolate or cheese.*"

I sighed, dreamily.

I'd trade tasty secrets for tasty cheese.

My witch rubbed her cheek against mine. "I'd be revealing *your* secret too."

My magic shook in distress, winding tighter inside me like it could hide. After all, that was what I'd always taught it. It existed to act like my witch's shadow.

Yet I'd reveal it for the sake of my witch.

The Great Satan feared no one apart from my witch's ma (and nobody could blame me for that because how would you feel if someone threatened to cut off *your* balls?).

I did fear, however, that Sin would rip me away from my witch.

She had all these other familiars now. On my whiskers, she could adopt Lucky, the unicorn, and have pooped glitter to look forward to every day or Precious, who no longer had an owner and was better trained than me.

A witch trained a dog, but a cat trained their witch.

I loved my witch, but if I needed to take the fall for this to save her and the shelter, which had long been her dream, then I would.

I was bad at taking orders but I was brilliant at protecting those who were mine.

"Nobody leave, while I start taking statements," Sin commanded. He straightened, clasping his hands behind his back. "I have a photographic memory, so if you *do* leave, then I'll have to draw an interesting inference from that." I smirked: *lie*. Plus, fair play to him. I liked how the Sheriff thought. "You…fluffy familiar thingy…"

He pointed at Precious.

Precious tilted his nose regally in the air. "*I'm a Pomeranian, laddy, descended from royalty and wolves.*"

Brilliant. A puppy with a Napoleon complex.

Sin blinked. "And I'm the Earl Sinclair, descended from the royal court and the wild silver dragons."

"*Good for you,*" Precious growled. "*But I didn't just call you a sparkly dragon thingy.*"

My witch giggled.

Sin looked stunned.

Without a new witch Mistress, Precious had gone rogue.

Why not speak telepathically to whomever he liked?

To my surprise, Sin's expression gentled. "My apologies, noble Precious. Could I entrust you to guard your Mistress' remains, while I carry out my investigation?"

Precious crept out from under the table and trotted to the ashes. When he sniffed at them sadly, however, he yelped. Then he rubbed his paw over his nose.

"What's wrong?" Sin demanded.

"*Hurts,*" Precious whimpered.

"*Like you've rubbed your nose over a stinging nettle?*" I asked.

Interesting…

Precious nodded.

When Sin shot me a sharp glance, I quailed.

Hmm, not the best way to prove my innocence. It sounded almost like I knew more than I was telling, which I now did.

I coughed. "*Lucky guess…?*"

"How about I do the talking?" My witch said in a tight voice.

"*You can try and see how it works out for you.*"

When Sin stalked towards the cottage, waving at us imperiously to follow him, my fur bristled. It was like he'd already claimed this as his territory

Except, this territory was mine.

I'd sprayed over it all to claim it.

If the dragon shifter wanted to challenge me for it, then we'd have to fight, and he'd have to get with the pissing. Sin looked like he was such a neat blueblood that he only used gold toilets.

On the other hand, with those muscles, he could defeat me with a single stamp of his boot.

Squish — no more Great Satan.

But then, my magic trumped his brawn.

"I'm getting the naughty vibes from you," my witch whispered, as we followed Sin to the cottage. She pushed open the heavy oak door and followed Sin in. "Just remember how serious this is."

"*On my tail, will you chill. I do. This isn't the first time that I've been accused of murder, remember?*"

Sin's shoulders stiffened.

"*The victims were three mice, two birds, and a shrew,*" my witch rushed to explain.

I smiled, smugly. "*Never proved, m'lord.*"

My witch passed Sin in the low-ceilinged lounge that was crammed with ancient charms, priceless relics, and my witch's wool.

Sin glanced around himself, horrified, at the piles of treasures...or rubbish.

But one man's rubbish was one demon kitten's treasure.

"Do you know how many of these are cursed?" Sin held his hands close to himself like he dreaded getting them dirty. "There are amulets, crystals, and...*is that a shrunken head?* Blast it all, these could contain the darkest magic."

My witch shrugged. "So, my great-aunt was a hoarder."

I rode on her shoulder like her white knight, bravely herding the fierce dragon up the oak spiral staircase, which was embossed with vines, apples, and pears. My heart clenched, and my pulse thundered in my ears, as she passed the first floor and headed straight for the attic.

The attic was the most magical part of the cottage.

It was also the domain of the Great Satan. My territory, magical playground, and nap zone.

Every familiar needed a nap zone.

Plus, it was home to the most dangerous potions, enchanted objects, and my computer.

Sin wasn't getting his dragony hands on any of them. They were possibly all as incriminating.

That's just our little secret, right?

Away with you, a magical kitten liked to experiment sort of like a mad scientist but more with cursed objects, herbs, or inventing new cryptocurrencies for a laugh.

My witch hesitated on the narrow landing outside the attic, before resting her hand on the sunflower, which was carved on the attic door. The door swung open at the gentle push of my magic through the sunflower, which was charmed to ward against intruders.

Like dragon shifters with flowery suits and silver eyes.

When Sin waltzed past us into the attic, I steadied myself with a deep sniff of the mingling oils that infused the beamed room: almond, clove, and sage.

It was the scent of both safety and freedom.

There was a high arched window, which looked out over the field behind the cottage, oiled floorboards (you needed a clean space to draw sigils for rituals), and crimson candles. The walls throbbed sapphire, adapting to my magic. In the far corner was a snuggly nest of blankets: my nap zone.

I hoped that Sin didn't notice my tiny plushie monkey with a forked tail, Hell, who my witch had knitted for me. I found his fiery red comforting, but Hell was mine, and I didn't want some sheriff touching my cuddle monkey.

Beneath the window was a stone lectern that held the most powerful object in my collection.

Of course, Sin marched straight towards it.

When I hissed, my witch placed me down on the floor, and I scrabbled, slipping on the floor to bite at Sin's trouser leg and hold him back.

A demon defended their territory.

Sin stopped and stared down at me. "Why do I appear to have a kitten attached to me?"

My witch shrugged. "It's how I get clients to adopt familiars. Oh no, you've found me out, Sheriff."

"Hilarious." Sin lifted his leg, and I dangled in the air. Then he glanced around the attic. "Why am I here?"

My witch's lips twitched. "Existential questions. You're handsome, loaded, and deep as well. What a catch."

"You think I'm handsome?"

My witch flushed.

I spat out Sin's trouser leg, tumbling to the floor.

My witch was rubbish at poker. Never show your hand first.

"Aren't we suspects?" My witch ventured. "Only I have a business to save…"

Sin pinked, coughing. "So, did you do it?"

I snickered. Inspector Morse had nothing to fear.

My witch crossed her arms. "Of course not. Did you?"

His eyes widened. "What?"

"Well, didn't you hate Marchbanks? You know, the witch who wanted the infamous pyromaniac collared."

Sin flinched and involuntarily touched his neck, before swallowing.

He curled his silver magic around himself, protectively. "It's wrong to talk badly of the dead, unless they've petitioned to have you transformed into your dragon form and tethered for an entire month on the village green, simply because of one loss of flame control. Then there was the matter of the scorched bench and…"

"*Aye, you sound practically pals.*" I glanced nervously at my lovely attic. "*You're not about to have a loss of flame control now, right?*"

Sin thought for a moment and then did the gesture for *fifty-fifty*. "Look, everybody hated Marchbanks. Witch Hollow is special. It's the most tolerant village in a paranormal world at war with itself. Where else can you imagine a werewolf chatting about pruning with a witch or a vampire falling in love with a mage? But the Inspectorate and the other petty founders who've sunk their claws into it want control. They're desperate not to allow everyone else free choice. Who wouldn't hate that?"

My witch's lips curled into a smile. "You're really not good at this whole authority Sheriff role are you? Sorry to break it to you, but you should be part of that establishment. I'm not sure that you should be sympathizing with the killer."

"*Is that like sympathy for the devil?*" I asked. "*Because I'm down with that.*"

Sin marched to my witch, and I tensed.

He gripped her chin; his eyes flared. "It may come as a surprise to you, but I'm more of an introvert than an extrovert. The Sheriff role is an inherited title. It's not like I applied for it. It just came to me along with the mansion."

"*British nepotism at its best*," I hissed.

Sin studied my witch. "The murder occurred at *your* event and it appeared *witchy* to me."

"*Witchy?*" My witch mouthed, offended.

Then her gaze became frosty. She ran a Repellent Charm along her skin (I smirked because I'd taught her that), and Sin gasped, pulling away from her.

"I thought that you didn't have magic," Sin accused.

"Firstly, how rude of you to eavesdrop on my telepathic conversations." My witch flounced towards the window, and her long hair whipped across Sin's chest. "Secondly, *barely* have magic. Still enough to surprise you."

"Evidently," he muttered, rubbing his hand ruefully.

Oh no, she wasn't about to show him my greatest treasure and my most personal possession...

My witch rested her hand on top of the large open book that sat on top of the lectern.

The leather-bound book had been given to my witch on her fifth birthday along with me, but it was really mine. It was a spell tome, filled with rituals, lists of ingredients, tricks, and hexes.

My witch called it The Demon Grimoire, but I

called it The Secret Diary of the All-Powerful Great Satan.

It was catchier.

My witch's ma had wondered whether her daughter was just a magical slow developer. She'd hoped that by giving her a demon familiar, it'd kick-start her power.

Instead, together we'd worked out a way to trick the world and save each other.

My witch should've been the one to fill in The Secret Diary. I'd set it with a charm, however, so that when I passed my paw over it, my witch's hand-writing would automatically scribble across the parchment.

Because I couldn't hold the pen myself, see, in my little paw. That'd be ridiculous.

My witch ran her hand over the Secret Diary lovingly. "Whatever killed Marchbanks took a high level of magical knowledge and power. I can sting you like a wasp, but not reduce you to ash. This book contains all the magic that we know, and we'll use it to help you. Isn't it obvious that I couldn't possibly have murdered that Inspector?"

Sin wandered to my diary, running his hands over it.

Bad touching...

I bounded to sit at the base of the lectern, and my

witch picked me up, sitting me on the ledge in front of the book.

"Ah ha!" Sin tapped the book. "How did your familiar know about the stinging nettle?"

I rested my teeth warningly on his finger, and he hurriedly removed it from the page. *"Brilliant deduction. Except, Precious hurt his nose, remember? Certain Fire Spells contain stinging nettle."*

"That's nice." Sin patted my head. *What? Was he patronizing the Great Satan?* "What spells need stinging nettle, Astra?"

My witch shot Sin a suitably withering glance. "Huh, let's ask the expert. Satan, why don't you show us what you know about Fire Spells?"

I grinned, as I held my paw over The Secret Diary, which glowed blue. It fluttered open, and Sin took a step back. Then he moved forward to peer at the page, which whirled to life with dancing flames. I'd always woven genuine spells into the pages, and each one was alive.

"Spices, herbs, and incenses can all contain the fierce powerful energy of fire." I vibrated with joy at the chance to lecture on my favorite subject: magic. All right then, my second favorite subject after *me.* *"They can cleanse and consecrate, as well as protect. But I'd bet my whiskers that the ones used on Marchbanks were to banish or exorcize because she was more of a demon than me."*

"Except that she didn't turn green and her head didn't spin, I'd have to agree." Sin stared at the flames, mesmerized.

His hand curled around the lectern like he was restraining himself from curling his fingers into the flames.

How hard was it for a dragon to push down his need to show his dragon form and resist fire for fear that he'd be collared? Probably, about as hard as it was for me to mask my power for fear that I'd be abandoned and caged.

I purred, rubbing my head against Sin's fingers.

Stop it instinctive purring sympathy.

Sin stared at me in shock, and I froze mid-purr.

I coughed. "*Just clearing my throat, see?*" Aye, they were totally tricked. "*The first Fire Spell that I cast was the Cheese Toastie Spell.*"

My witch clapped her hands in delight. "I love that one! Mum doesn't believe in toasties on principle. *Ehm*, she doesn't believe in a lot of things on principle. Anyway, I'd sneak sandwiches up into the bedroom for midnight feasts, and Satan had worked out how to melt the cheese."

I waved my paw over the page and the words danced to form the correct spell in my witch's scrawled handwriting:

MY BRILLIANT CHEESE TOASTIE SPELL

Pepper
Chilli
Oil of Abramelin
Snapdragon
Marigold
Holly
Stinging Nettle

Use the Ritual of Mars and the spirit of the sun

Spells were recipes.

I'd make an excellent chef, as long as diners didn't mind fur in their food.

"So, that's why you recognized the stinging nettle," Sin said, thoughtfully. Then his gaze hardened. "You do realize that all this shows is that *you* knew how to explode Marchbanks?"

Whoops…

"Don't you see?" My witch glanced at The Secret Diary with the respect that it deserved. "A Grimoire will only respond to the most magically powerful creature in the room. It should be me or perhaps, you. *But it worked for Satan.* I don't have the power to wield fire as a weapon like this."

When Sin's eyes darkened, my breath became ragged. I tumbled backward into the safety of my witch's arms.

Why did the Sheriff look so much scarier all of a sudden?

"You're quite right." Sin's hard gaze met mine. "You've proved that your familiar is powerful, if he has more magic even than me. He's also loyal and clearly loves you. I'd guess that he'd do anything for you. Perhaps, even kill to protect you and this shelter. Congratulations, you've just made Satan the chief suspect."

CHAPTER FIVE

Evermore Farm, Witch Hollow

ASTRA

The opening event of my magical shelter hadn't gone *exactly* as I'd hoped. I mean, it'd ended up with more dead witches than adopted demon familiars.

Yet didn't all businesses have teething problems?

Setting my kitten up as the chief suspect hadn't been my finest moment. But then, I hadn't been taught *how to act innocent when being interrogated by a gorgeous dragon shifter Sheriff* by the fancy tutors that Morgan had employed.

And Sin *was* gorgeous with shoulders that just

begged for my fingers to trail over them, even if he was an elitist snob.

Who'd also protected me.

I sighed, burrowing further down into my sagging bed with its rich blue silk covers. My bedroom at Evermore farm was surrounded by mahogany alcoves of books. The reassuring scent of books mingled with sweet rose.

I stared up at the glass ceiling. This was my favorite room in the house. I could lie here and watch the stars in the night-time sky.

It was like being connected to the universe and its deep magics. Was this what it was like all the time for Satan?

Yet was I powerful enough to keep my familiars safe, alone in the village of Witch Hollow?

Did Morgan want me to stay and work in her business because she'd feared something like this?

My jaw clenched.

Sweet Hecate, I wasn't going back.

I'd show them all that it wasn't about how much magic you possessed, but rather your determination that counted.

After all, I'd convinced Sin not to arrest Satan and haul him off to some kind of kitten jail with nothing but the power of my words (begging still counted).

Clever words like: *it's nothing but circumstan-*

tial...look at those cute little whiskers...please with a cherry on the top?

Yet that didn't stop Satan being top of the Most Likely to Have Burned Marchbanks to Ash List.

So, I'd just have to prove that he didn't do it.

I traced my fingers over the glittery writing on the front of my sapphire pajamas: **What's Up, Witches?**

Bonnie Tyler's power ballad "Total Eclipse of the Heart" wailed like a love song to a vampire through the room.

I grimaced. So, Satan was still sulking then.

To be fair, I had revealed his secret in order to protect us both, and instead, we were in as much danger as before. "Total Eclipse of the Heart" was on my Starlight Break Up Playlist. Satan was a cat king at sulking revenge.

Of course, if Satan wanted to play that game...

I twisted to Satan, who was still hiding beneath the sheets. He snuggled next to his tiny monkey plushie that I'd knitted for him. His large emerald eyes shone up at me, and almost vanished my resolve. He could get away with anything when he looked at me like that.

Except, he knew it.

I shivered at the thought of silver eyes looking at me in the same loving way. Sin would demand, rather than beg.

Wouldn't he...?

Bluebloods were taught from the cradle to demand their milk delivered on silver trays by servants.

I'd imagine.

Okay, no more weird imagining.

Instead, I broke into an off-key rendition of "Wrecking Ball" that clashed with "Total Eclipse" in a satisfying way.

Witching heavens, I could weaponize this.

Satan yowled, drawing further under the covers. I blocked his retreat, however, and pulled him out, as he wriggled. Conceding defeat, he shut off the music with a wave of his paw.

I grinned, before I crooned a final line of the song. Then I lay back in what I admit was blessed silence, positioning Satan on my chest. He kneaded me like even after all these years, he was still hopeful to stimulate milk and then circled round, before curling into a ball.

I stroked over his ear. It was a shame that his hat had been destroyed. I'd knit him a new one tomorrow because he'd been devastated to lose it, which had been a surprise.

I loved to make him happy, however, so I'd make sure he didn't go without a hat from now on. Perhaps, I could add a scarf?

Sorry you're a suspect but look: new hat!

I ran my hand along my copy of *Pride and Preju-*

dice, which I'd been trying to read. Darcy was a book boyfriend that I both wanted to hex and spank.

He reminded me of Sin.

Yet I was too distracted to read and too anxious to sleep.

Cauldrons and candles, it wasn't simply my shelter being shut down (although, what'd happen to all the familiars who I loved then?). It was losing Satan because his powers had been revealed.

Since I was five years old that'd been my worst fear.

And it was all happening because of a Witch Inspector. Ironic that I hated her but I'd have to solve her murder.

"*You're thinking too loudly,*" Satan said, sleepily.

He raised his head to meet my gaze through slitted eyes.

I snorted. "Usually, you say that I don't think enough."

"*I would never...*" Satan smirked. "*Aye, that sounds like me. Worry more quietly. I don't know how your singing torture didn't wake the ball of fluff.*"

I glanced at the end of the bed.

Marchbanks' puppy familiar, Precious, curled like a fox wrapped in a bundle of fluff on a satin pillow.

Toads and frogs, he was tiny.

When I'd settled the rest of the familiars away for the night — the larger familiars in the adapted stables, the mid-size in the spare bedrooms, the birds in the aviary, apart from the night birds like the owls who were out partying, carrying messages for fictional wizards, or whatever they got up to, and the mice sized in shoe boxes filled with fluff — I hadn't been able to leave Precious by himself.

Marchbanks might've been a horrible witch, but she'd been Precious' witch. And demons were possessive and protective. He had to be suffering.

So, he wouldn't be alone.

Satan had, of course, hissed his outrage at another familiar taking his place on our bed (because *possessive*).

Satan had graciously compromised with the pillow at the end of the bed.

When the door creaked open, letting in a sliver of light from the landing, I stiffened.

Then a burst of glitter blasted through the room. I spluttered, wiping it off my face.

Okay, nasty.

"Lucky," I gasped.

The miniature unicorn trotted into the room. The demon familiar that I'd inherited from Ursula was midnight black with a twisted silver horn. His eyes were like swirling obsidian pools to hell.

Not that I'd tell him that. He'd love it too much.

Plus, was he now wearing eyeliner and black lipstick...?

"*This bed is full up. No more room for snuggling imposters.*" Satan's eyes narrowed. "*Why are you here?*"

Lucky plopped down onto the oriental rug beside the bed. I was amazed that he'd had the energy to even walk to my room. He'd only managed to fit in one snooze today because of the opening.

He must be exhausted.

Lucky's lips curled back, and Satan sank his claws tighter into me like he was hooking himself in for safety. "*The freaks come out at night.*"

I raised an unimpressed eyebrow. "Well, it's past the freak's bedtime."

Lucky's eyes swirled faster. "*Look me in the eyeliner and say that.*"

I *eep*ed.

Satan wagged his tail. "*Lay off the prince of Hell act and make yourself useful. You heard about the murder.*"

Lucky's horn glowed. "*Lucky that I always wear black.*" Then he closed his eyes, before slurring, "*Whoever burned her must've wanted everyone to see.*"

Then he was snoring.

I jolted.

The Goth unicorn had a point. Perhaps, the public aspect of the murder hadn't been an accident but deliberate.

But why?

Maybe, I shouldn't concentrate on simply proving Satan's innocence but working out who in this village had wanted to publicly kill Marchbanks. Whoever it was, I had a serious grudge with them myself for ruining my opening.

"*That was creepy as always.*" Satan shuddered. "*The fine thing about other demon familiars, is that it reminds you how brilliant the Great Satan is.*"

"Really?"

Satan glanced at me hopefully. "*And means that you forget about wee naughtiness like the time I set up a twitter profile called @RealSabrinaWitch and posted all your pictures.*"

I froze. "You never told me about that."

He shot me an innocent look. "*Didn't I? Why don't we simply say that I'm telling you now and leave it at that? You have over a million followers.*"

"Wow, that's..." I shook my head. "...not the point. I want it deleted."

"*Done.*" When Satan edged closer to me and rubbed his head against my chin, I knew that I was about to be outmaneuvered. "*Quid pro quo. If I delete it, then you talk this over with your gran.*"

I frowned. "You're not Hannibal Lecter."

Satan did a disturbingly good Hannibal impression, before snickering. "*Get on with you, Clarice, you know that your gran has the badassery to deal with this. You'll never sleep until you chat with her.*"

"I'll never sleep *once* I've spoken to her," I grumbled.

But Satan was right.

My gran, Zosia, had raised me, since Morgan had been too busy running her demon familiar empire and other wickedness. She was a super powerful witch. Zosia was old-fashioned, but there was nobody better to have in your corner (or to ask for candy because she could magic the best ones from around the world).

I loved her, and she'd proved her own...unique...style of love many times.

Even if I did prefer not talking to her face to face.

Satan winked at me in victory, before creating a portal above me with a flick of his claw.

"Not with visuals," I gasped.

What would Zosia think of these pajamas? And why was it that I still cared about things like that at my age? I flushed. *I still cared.*

Satan did a kitteny shrug, before fogging the portal.

I ran my fingers nervously through my tangled hair, as I waited, listening to the tinny ring.

At last Zosia's tired but sharp voice demanded, "What's Satan done this time? He's finally led you to your death, hasn't he?"

Satan sat up in delight like it was the best compliment that he'd ever received.

"Not unless this is Zombie Me calling you." I patted my check. "Nope, just boring old witchy me. Sorry for calling so late, Gran."

Zosia huffed. "That's what a zombie would say to trick me."

"I'm pretty sure it'd be more like *uhhhh*...."

"Now, Astra, I know that I didn't bring you up to be prejudiced like that." My cheeks pinked at her censor. She hadn't lost her touch at scolding. "Just tell me that you still have all ten fingers and other things people are meant to ask."

"I think that's babies, but yeah, I'm fine."

"Then, sorry if this sounds abrupt, but why are you portal calling me at the owl side of midnight?"

"Oh, is it that late? *Whoops*." There went my blush again.

Satan's smile was sly. *He'd known*, the wicked little demon.

All of a sudden, it was harder to tell Zosia about what'd happened today. She'd supported my move into Evermore Farm against Morgan's wishes, and I wanted to prove to her that she'd been right to believe in me.

"Did you burn down the cottage?" Zosia asked.

I chewed on my hair. "Not quite."

"You're pregnant?"

Silver eyes, fluttering magic, and orchids...

"W-why would you ask... I don't even... Not that I wouldn't like to become a mum when I'm ready because I *would* just not until I have the business sorted and..."

"I'll take that as a *no*, shall I?" Zosia said, drily.

"*I don't know how we should take it.*" Satan chuckled.

"We could try playing Ten Questions, or you could simply tell me," Zosia suggested.

"Today was my opening event," I explained, "and I've been thinking hard about my life." *Here goes...* "A witch was murdered at the opening, I want to solve Dad's disappearance, and I met someone."

I learned from Satan to always mix bad news in with slightly *less* bad news, *and* something unexpected.

Satan gave me an impressed nod. "*The apprentice surpasses her master.*"

Silence.

Okay, say something...*anything...*

"*You've met someone?* You do remember that you're supposed to wait until your mother makes an official matching with a suitable boy. You're already years past the usual date most witches settle down because you've rejected every match that she sets you up with. I have to admit that I'll be pleased if you've found someone for yourself because the latest boy that she's found for you, Cyril, may be from the best coven but he's so shy that he stares at his feet like they're tattooed with the Sphinx's Spell. Go on then, tell me about your new beau."

I winced, staring into the swirling fog like I'd be able to see Zosia through it. I told her about a murder, and she picked me *dating* as the more startling statement.

Worse, was the information that Morgan was trying to match me with someone named *Cyril*. Most witches had arranged marriages, but I'd been dodging that fate for years.

Weirdly defensive, I found myself wetting my lips. "I bet poor Cyril's family trained him to act like that. We treat our men in the covens as badly as we treat our familiars. You know that's why I haven't wanted a matching. Those men didn't choose me."

Had Dad, Tadeas, run away, rather than disappeared?

My guts roiled. I'd asked myself that many times, as I'd grown older and learned the truth of witch society.

But would Tadeas have run and left me behind?

I knew that Tadeas loved me. He'd shown me kindness every day and told me every night, as he'd tucked me in to sleep.

I'd only been tiny when he'd vanished but I still remembered that.

Yet why had I talked about Sin like we'd gone out for coffee, rather than an interrogation?

Sin probably hated me. I seriously doubted that he was lying in bed penning me poems or doing something more intimate…

Bad brain.

"He's tall." Why did this pretend relationship feel more real the more that I defended it? *Still, it wasn't a lie.* "Dark-haired." Also, not a lie. "Stupidly handsome," *Hecate's honest truth...* "and from one of the village's local covens."

Hex my lying ass now.

Zosia's non-paranormal prejudice only went so far. I already had to chat about a murder with her. I didn't want to bring up that the fake boyfriend was a dragon shifter.

"That's wonderful," Zosia exclaimed. "I don't care what your mum says, you're a catch." *Wait, what?* "I can't wait to meet the fine young man. What House does he...?"

"Murder!" *I didn't just shout that did I?*

"*You're adorable when you're all subtle*," Satan murmured.

"I mean, not now...not again...this morning at the event. Now Satan and I are suspects because it was some kind of Fire Spell or Hex. Anyway, we're implicated because the victim was the Inspector who could've failed the business."

"It's simple." Zosia yawned like she dealt with murder every day. Of course, I'd yet to discover what her true job was. *It was very hush-hush*, was all she'd ever admit. *Did witch spies say that in real life?* "If the authorities are dim enough to think that you're responsible, then you solve it for them. Didn't I teach you well enough? Get your claws in the investigation by any means necessary. Don't be led by whoever's in charge; you lead them. I remember your familiar was always excellent at such things."

I curled my hand around Satan protectively.

Did Zosia guess about Satan's powers or just his scheming?

Satan nudged me with his head. "*Your gran is fiendish, ruthless, and right.*"

"Thanks, Gran," I said, softly. "I love you."

"I've always believed in you, even during your teenage soapbox stage and that was so annoying I wanted to hex you myself. Oh, you haven't grown out of it yet, have you?"

Satan burst out laughing.

I tapped him on his whiskery nose. "Hey, do you want me to swap your snuggle position with Precious or the unicorn of darkness?" That sobered up Satan quickly. "Thanks, for the advice. Night."

"You've got this," Zosia said. "Night."

As the portal faded, Satan cuddled down as if to be

certain that his spot was claimed. Yet I wasn't certain that I *did* have this.

Tomorrow, I had to persuade my fake haughty boyfriend, who believed that my kitten familiar could be a murderer, to let me investigate at his side.

I wouldn't allow any of my familiars down because they relied on me.

Yet as Zosia had made clear, I had to tame a dragon to catch a killer.

CHAPTER SIX

Silver Hall, Witch Hollow

ASTRA

Why was I as nervous to see my dragon shifter again, as I was to catch a killer?

Bubbling cauldrons, could it be because Gran had suggested I take up dragon taming?

And why was I thinking of him as *my* shifter?

I shifted from foot to foot on the sweeping marble steps of Silver Hall, Sin's Georgian mansion and the ancestral home of his family. The hall had columns that were as straight as Sin's back and hundreds of gleaming windows.

It was handsome, immaculate, and majestic...*like Sin.*

I took a deep breath.

The soft tinkling of the fountain behind me was almost too calming. I glanced down the long gravel driveway. The fountain was made up of three stone dragons, which gushed water out of their mouths like flames. It was surrounded by manicured gardens and oaks.

I winced at the sight of the broken fence through to my jungle of a property. It was the only thing to mar Silver Hall's perfection like a chipped tooth in a handsome face.

Sweet Hecate, was that how Sin saw me and my familiars?

A chipped tooth?

I grimaced, running my fingers through my wild hair. I'd pinned it down with three cat clips this morning, which had nothing to do with a certain Sheriff with smoldering silver eyes.

Obviously.

Satan sat on the step next to me like he owned Silver Hall.

Like he owned the world.

I swallowed. Witching heavens, I was never entirely sure whether Satan actually did.

Satan looking up at me with a sardonic expression (and for a cat, he pulled that off.). "*Take it easy. You look beautiful, as always. If you want to mate with the shifter, he'll fall to his knees. Then you can provide me* with witchy shifter babies, who'll be mine for…totally innocent purposes."

"That's not…there'll be no…he's just my fake boyfriend…*mate*?" I flushed. I didn't even know where to start with Satan's plans, but the handing over of my imaginary *witchy shifter* babies was as good a place as any. "And any babies will be mine."

Satan pouted. "*Spoilsport. Anyway, according to that wildlife documentary, which you didn't shut off before my furry arse had nightmares for weeks, you need to mate before there are babies.*"

He shuddered.

Satan had been so proud about his fellow cats, the tigers, right up until the male had pinned down the female. He'd hissed furiously that *he'd been killing her and why were none of her pals helping?*

It hadn't been the ideal way to teach sex education, but in my defense, I'd never expected to need to teach Satan. I'd stopped him being neutered, but demon familiars didn't get frisky.

I paled. *Hecate help my descendants, let that be true…*

When Satan was older, if he fathered litters of little Satans to follow in his footsteps, then there'd be no stopping him.

He always was one for long-term scheming.

I raised my hand to knock on the intimidating front door.

My guts roiled with a squirmy sensation of wrongness like just before I started a period. I ignored it. Except, I usually chose to believe the night before a period started that my bloating was because I'd eaten too much pasta. That'd end with Satan frantically casting a Banish Period spell to save me eternal embarrassment.

I'd allowed him as much cheese as he could scoff (and witches above, that was a lot), when he'd invented *that* spell.

Why did I feel like this morning I had the bloated stomach as warning but was choosing to ignore it?

Did that mean disaster was only hours away and this time, Satan wouldn't simply be able to banish it away?

I straightened my shoulders, even as my pulse thundered.

I'd do this for my familiars and Satan.

I *rap — rap — rapped* on Sin's door like I was here by invitation of the Dragon Empress herself.

Satan slashed his claws through the air. "*Swish-crack. On my whiskers, you go tame the dragon.*"

"Not helping," I muttered.

"*Not trying to.*"

I held my breath, as I heard footsteps on the other side of the door.

Any moment now…

86

Surely, an earl would have servants. Would a butler in black tie welcome us in and introduce us?

The door violently swung open, and Sin blocked the entrance, studying me blankly.

Frogs and toads, had he always been so tall?

My throat was suddenly dry. I wiped my palms down my dress.

Slow romantic music drifted from inside. Was he holding a party or perhaps, a *party for two*? And why did my heart clench at that thought?

Sin's expression tightened for a moment, before it became shuttered. "Not today, thank you."

I stared at him in amazement.

Crash — Sin slammed shut the heavy door in my face.

I froze. "Well, that happened."

Satan stalked to the door. "*The Great Satan shall curse him to be shown the least relevant Internet searches forever…*"

"Tempting. But as he's Sheriff, he may need to explore the non-magical world on occasion. Anyway, I still have the might of my tiny fist."

I banged on the door again and I didn't stop.

Zosia hadn't raised me to be a quitter.

What a shame if I was spoiling the mood of Sin's date…

When Sin swung open the door for a second time, his eyes flashed. "What on my wings are you doing?

I've already let your demon familiar go, when by rights, I should've caged him."

"*Just try it*," Satan hissed.

"Oh joy." Sin adjusted his cuffs. "I can still hear your pussy."

I snorted. "I seriously hope that you can't."

Because right now, with Sin standing there looking just a *little* ruffled (and was it weird how much I wanted to mess up his immaculate suit and hair?), it'd probably give my feelings away…

Yet he had some female dragon shifter in there who probably didn't have mud smeared down her dress, hadn't broken his property, or invited him to events with murders.

The murder was the biggie.

Sin reddened. "Your *cat*."

I smirked. "I know."

Sin leaned against the door frame. "I'm busy here." *Yeah, busy kissing.* "I spent all last night investigating." *Your dragony girlfriend.* "I didn't sleep a single wink." *Too much information.* "My brother has been scolding me for the last hour." I wrinkled my nose. Okay, now this was becoming too kinky for me. "He's the Duke in our Oxford Court, and if I don't solve the case, then it looks bad on him and our family name. I have responsibilities, you know."

The case… Okay, that made more sense.

"So, you need our help." I smiled, brightly.

Sin arched his elegant brow. "I really don't. Witches have refused to help me since I took up this role. Letting them close has ended in nothing but petitions to treat me like a beast. Why are you different?"

Wow, that was one serious chip on his shoulder.

My brow furrowed. "Trust me, I am."

He huffed. "Excuse me if I don't feel inclined to trust murder suspects. Even if I wish that I could."

For a moment, there was something vulnerable and hopeful in his expression.

"Let us be your helpers. It's my duty to prove that Satan's innocent," I insisted.

Sin's eyes narrowed. "What do you know about duty? I'd imagine that your most demanding one is defleaing your spoiled kitten."

"*I don't have fleas*," Satan gasped, outraged. "*I have* demon *fleas*."

Sin shivered like he was imagining those *demon fleas* hopping down his spine, before he tried to slam the door again. But I jammed it open with my foot, and his eyes widened in shock.

As Zosia said: *lead and don't be led, by any means necessary.*

Sin hunched his shoulders, closing his eyes in frustration. Then he threw open the door, prowling back inside.

Result!

Satan spun in a victory dance and then trotted after Sin.

I smiled and followed them both, staring around in amazement at the luxurious marble foyer. The high roof was painted with grand battles between gold, silver, and bronze dragons. The walls were gilt silver but rippled like they were alive. I'd bet that even a single one of the antiques, which encircled the room, were worth more than my entire farm. A vast staircase that looked like it'd been painted in silver swept down from the higher floors.

My breath caught.

It was the most beautiful but also *coldest* house that I'd ever seen.

I peered around me. "Sorry for interrupting. So, where is she?"

Sin crossed his arms. "Who?"

I bit my lip. "Your..." Did dragons call it bonded or…witching heavens, *was he married?* "Lady friend."

"*Weak*." Satan chuckled.

Sin cleared his throat. "I don't have a lady friend here or anywhere, if that's what you're asking."

"Who's asking?" I said, sharply.

"You…?" Sin replied, confused.

"I can confirm that there's no one here but His Lordship," a suave English voice answered from the walls.

I jumped at the same time as Satan, who'd been exploring the room and sniffing at the antiques. His fur bristled, until he looked like an adorable spiky ball.

"Thanks for making sure my virtue and good name are safe, Draco." Sin patted the wall. "Draco is the magical AI Butler who serves me. It's an ancient name that means *dragon*."

I tilted my head. "You're a *Harry Potter* fan, huh? You're clearly a Slytherin."

"Do you wish me to eject the unwelcome guests, Your Lordship?" Draco asked.

How was it possible for such a simple question to be tinged with enough menace to be a threat?

Draco was badass.

The air crackled with wards, energizing to repel me. In turn, Satan glowed blue in defense.

This was not turning out how I'd hoped, but then, I hadn't been expecting to face a psycho AI butler.

Sin held up his hands like the magnanimous landowner. "Not just now, Draco."

"Very well," Draco said, sounding disappointed and a touch disapproving. "I stand ready."

When Sin stepped closer and his silver magic wrapped around me, *I* wasn't ready for the intense scent of myrrh or the way that my pulse fluttered wildly in my neck. "Why were you concerned that I'd be with a lover?"

His gaze was searching.

I waved my arms around like I could catch at the music: Taylor Swift's intimate indie-folk ballad "Lover" with its bass riff and booming snare echoed through the foyer like a heartbeat.

Sin's eyes widened comically large, and he stumbled back from me. "Draco, shut off the music."

"Whatever you say, Your Lordship."

"I forgot that was playing." Sin ran his finger around the lip of a vase like he'd find inspiration there. "I don't normally listen to that type of music but I needed something to help me concentrate, and it's just so…"

"*Catchy.*" Satan darted to Sin, winding between his legs and purring, like he'd found a new pal in their shared Taylor Swift embarrassment. "*I have your back, big boy.*"

Sin stepped back from Satan, staring in horror at the hairs that were now on his trousers. "Never call me that again."

"*Noted but no promises.*"

Satan wound around Sin's legs again, rubbing himself with great relish against his trousers. Then he darted back to me with his tail high like he'd just staked his claim.

"Where are your manners, Your Lordship? Your brother has spoken with me about your need to make more friendships and that means proper welcoming etiquette," Draco chastised.

A drinks cabinet shaped like a dragon's egg clattered magically into the foyer with brandy glasses ready. I took a deep sniff of the rich, fruity scent.

I hadn't felt like a drink before I'd walked over here, but Hecate above, I did now.

Before I could reach for the glass, however, Sin sighed.

"I don't care what my brother says. He knows that I get all…flamey…when I drink. Take the blasted stuff away. Astra isn't that kind of guest."

I wasn't sure whether I was offended that Sin didn't consider me the *kind of guest* who was served the good sort of brandy or pleased that he had the restraint not to lose his flame control.

"My apologies, Your Lordship," Draco didn't sound sorry, rather more like Satan, after he'd used up my best shampoo washing his fur, "but I didn't realize that she was the *other* kind of guest."

A bed slammed down between us, which was complete with silver sheets and pillows. By Sin's shocked attempt to straighten the covers, I'd bet that it was *his* bed.

"Draco, you're dismissed." A muscle twitched in Sin's jaw.

"As you wish," Draco drawled.

Wow, butlers with attitude.

Sin scrambled over the bed, which now divided us, before straightening out his jacket…like he hadn't just needed to scramble over his own bed.

"*Ehm*, can we be awfully English about this and act like nothing happened? You know, pretend that we didn't even see the really embarrassing thing that happened in front of our own eyes?"

…by all means necessary…

My lips quirked. "Tell me about these *other kind of guests*. Do you get them so often that you have a whole protocol for summoning your bed?"

Sin opened and shut his mouth a couple of times, before he spluttered. "Of course not… I never get them…or just the usual number of…and whatever is the usual number, anyway? I mean…"

"*On my whiskers, you should try out for the Oxford Debate Championships*." Satan sat on Sin's polished shoe, and he winced. "*Now be quiet and listen to my witch. She needs you, and I don't think you're totally useless, so you'll have to do*."

"Thank you," Sin said, drily.

This was it. You could lead a dragon to water, but you couldn't make it drink. Actually, I doubt you could even lead it, which is what I was attempting.

Here went nothing…

"You inherited your role as Sheriff, which is sucky because my mum also tried to force me into the family business," I said. Sin studied me; his expression gentled with interest. "Now if you want, you've inherited us."

Sin took a sharp intake of breath, and his pupils dilated. He stepped towards me, gripping me by the shoulders. Satan came along for the ride, clinging onto his foot by his claws.

"Dragons are possessive." Sin's tongue darted out to lick his plush lips, and I couldn't look away. "As much as you're both valuable, this is too soon to take our relationship to such a—"

"*Whoa*, Mr. Commitment." I batted Sin away, and his eyes flashed with hurt. Okay, that was a punch to the gut. Wasn't he only supposed to be my *fake* boyfriend? When had it become real? "*For the investigation.* Satan and I are solving it with or without you, so we may as well solve it together. I have to show that he's innocent, and I have to protect my business."

"I knew that," Sin whispered, turning away his head. "Just dragon instincts again."

I assessed him, speculatively. *Was it true?*

"*So, if I drink all the cream, do I get away with saying it was just kitten instincts? Or push Precious off the bed? Or magic all the mice in the world into zombie mice and then use them to—*"

"No," Sin and I chorused at the same time.

"*Double standards*," Satan muttered.

"Stop giving my demon familiar ideas." I perched on the edge of Sin's bed, which made him stiffen.

What'd happen if I rolled around on it and messed up all the sheets? "The murder happened on my property, and Satan's name won't be cleared, until we find out who really did this. Maybe you don't know how the witch world works, but demon familiars have zero rights. If my mum decides that he's dangerous, even though he was given to me, she could take him away and have him destroyed. She could even take away all my familiars."

Satan mewled and covered his head with his paws.

What I'd said had been true but I regretted voicing it instantly.

To my shock, Sin reached down and picked up Satan, holding him awkwardly in one large hand, as if he'd never held an animal before and more like Satan was a baby. To my equal shock, Satan allowed it, basking in the attention.

"There, there." Sin patted Satan on the head. "I won't allow that to happen. I promise, I'll keep you safe." Satan shot me a smug look like he'd known all along that he'd be the one getting the cuddles. To be honest, he was cute. "You're suspects, and so I'm breaking all sorts of rules by allowing this but I'm also a suspect and so is pretty much everybody else. Also, I'm the Sheriff, as I reminded my brother this morning. If nothing else, it means that I get to run this my way."

"You rebel," I grinned.

He arched his brow. "More like outcast but rebel sounds cooler." He hugged Satan closer to him, and I loved the protective way that he glanced between us. I found that I didn't mind the thought of him inheriting us both. "I took statements from everyone at the event who had opportunity, motive, and means. I made a short list, but it's not that short."

"*Everybody hated Marchbanks, right?*" Satan said. "*So, it's a question of who had the greatest reason to hate her.*"

Sin huffed. "Besides you?"

"*Besides me.*"

Sin strolled to the door. "We'd better go together to Witch Hollow and find out." He bit his lip, ducking his head. "I haven't been there since the whole *scorching the bench* incident. You become known as a recluse mainly by being one."

Well, that wasn't right at all. My familiars didn't deserve to be rejected for who they were and neither did Sin.

I strolled to Sin and clasped his hand. He stared at our joined hands in surprise, before his fingers squeezed mine. "I've been so busy fixing up the farm for the opening that I haven't been into the main village either. So, why don't we brave it together."

His lips twitched. "If you've never seen Witch Hollow, then you'll be in for a surprise."

Uh-oh…

My guts roiled. *Sweet Hecate, I'd known not to ignore my bloated stomach warning.*

My fingers tightened around Sin's. Perhaps, it was time to show him that I could lead?

"Satan, why don't you take us to the village?" I said.

Satan nodded.

When Sin's gaze locked on mine, my breath caught at the depth of trust in his eyes.

Satan's magic glowed like a blue haze, enveloping our little group.

Sin howled, Satan cackled, and I held on for the ride, as we magically transported to Witch Hollow.

CHAPTER SEVEN

The Cemetery, Witch Hollow

SATAN

My demon side thrilled at my witch's new mate's howl, as I transported us together in the blink of a cat's eye from Silver Hall to the village of Witch Hollow. If you had no experience of transportation, then it was like being unwoven and then knitted together, just with a stitch or two missing...

I cackled, landing on my feet beneath a twisted yew tree.

Scream before the Great Satan, bow down and...

Hold on, I got carried away there. Let's keep that just between us, right?

It was a fine thing to flex both my demon and magical muscles, rather than wearing silly hats and sharing a bathroom with ferret twins.

Away with you, I knew how to perch on a toilet, even if I'd fallen in once or twice and had to be pulled out by a laughing witch. Toilet water didn't count as taking a bath, no matter what my witch insisted. I suspected that she just wanted to hoard her luxury hair products.

I'd watched the adverts, however, and I knew that I was *worth it.*

I tossed my head, preening.

Sin crashed onto his arse in a patch of mud. He grimaced, inspecting his dirty suit. I could cast a Cleansing Hex but I wouldn't. His trousers were covered in my hairs (as it should be), and he now looked as messy as my witch.

Like a matching pair.

That was a fine sight.

I smiled, as my witch *popped* out of the air onto a low tomb. She casually sprawled on it like a bed.

She had class.

I glanced with interest around the cemetery, which was on the edge of the village, with its tumbledown gravestones, marble mausoleums, and tangle of trees. I wrinkled my nose at the moist mossy, *rotting* stink.

I grinned with more than a hint of my tiny fangs at

the deadly plants that grew between the graves — deadly nightshade, wolfsbane, and hemlock — which I could use in my experiments. Brewing potions was no different to cooking. It was like taking recipes for brownies, see, but adding a dash of hemlock, instead of chocolate chips.

Of course, the potion could then control the...victim's...mind or make them feel like they were flying. I'd never heard of a brownie that could do that.

Okay, the humans *claimed* to have created one. But I didn't believe it.

Yet if this many poisonous plants grew here, then any magical creature could brew whatever they liked.

Brilliant.

Witch Hollow was a village of trusting supernaturals, which offered me an ideal opportunity, but also meant that I'd have to make certain that my witch didn't become one of them.

I'd do anything to protect her.

Since my witch had settled in Evermore, she hadn't left the farm. She'd been too busy fixing it up and saving abandoned, unwanted, and mistreated familiars.

It was her mission.

I respected that, but she did appear to get on better with familiars than people.

Familiars were superior, after all.

I'd used The Secret Diary in the attic to figure out some brilliant Dark Magic to make sure that my witch had everything she needed with the Deliver me Anything Spell.

My witch had almost rumbled me, after she'd collapsed exhausted one day. Lucky had been so worried that he'd even woken up from his nap and licked her face. My witch had only giggled and gasped that she'd needed a sugar lift. Less than half an hour later, a blond-haired Omega werewolf had puffed his way up to her with a bemused expression, holding out a single chocolate cupcake on a golden platter.

My witch had turned a fierce stare on me, but as soon as she'd moaned in chocolate heaven, munching the cupcake, she'd forgotten my naughtiness.

Once the Omega had handed her a steaming cup of coffee as well, I'd known that I'd been safe.

Victory for the kitten!

Sin climbed to his feet, brushing down his suit like that'd help him bring back his dignity. *Too late.* "Never do that again."

My ear twitched. "*No deal. That was fun.*"

Sin sighed. "Then never do that without warning me first."

Both my ears twitched. "*Acceptable counteroffer.*"

My witch glanced around the cemetery curiously. "I know that we're investigating a death but Marchbanks was reduced to ashes. There's no corpse to dig up or..."

"Before you offer any more horrifying suggestions," Sin paled, "there'll be no autopsy or even necromancy style investigations." He shuffled his feet. "There are no strict rules to being Sheriff. Mostly, the different supernaturals police themselves, and I don't have to do anything. It's why I've been stranded out here in Witch Hollow, which is different. Their unique *living together* philosophy means that I have more of a job. Even then, it's as if the Mayor wants me to keep everyone in line just by being all..." He flared out his magic, and his eyes flashed. "*Rrrrooooarr*! You see?"

I shrank back, hiding behind a moss-covered gravestone. The big dragon shifter was scary, underneath his charm.

My witch, however, only cushioned her arms on her elbows. "I thought that you were banned from the village because of the *rrrrooooarr*?"

Sin shivered like her reply roar had been a mating call.

He wet his lips. "Let nobody say that witch society is fair. Mostly, I was called in as the..."

He pinked.

"*Muscle*?" I suggested. "*Security? Brawn?*"

Sin clenched his jaw. "It certainly wasn't for my *brains* to solve complex investigations. You made me realize that I shouldn't simply accept the role, however, as other's have prescribed it for me. I'm the Sheriff—"

"*And now you're going to clean up this town.*" I held my tail high. My witch snickered. "Along with your posse, Satan, and—"

"How can I clean it up, when you've made me dirtier than I've ever been?" Sin pulled a silk handkerchief out of his pocket, wiping at his palms compulsively. When he met my witch's teasing gaze, he swallowed. "In an entirely non-euphemistic way, obviously."

"Of course." My witch slipped off the tomb, before sauntering to Sin. She took his palm between her hands. "Huh, this bothers you?"

"I do have a reputation."

"I know. I heard it from Marchbanks."

Low blow...

Sin's eyes flared. "If you judged everyone by what Marchbanks thought of them, then you'd hate the entire village."

"I don't hate anyone." My witch warmed a simple Cleansing Spell across Sin's skin, dispelling the mud. "With the possible exception of people who bully familiars and queue jumpers."

Sin's expression softened. "Thank you."

My witch held onto his hand way longer than she needed to, stroking over his knuckles with her thumb.

My tail lashed.

Hey, cat down here not getting stroked...

I meowed.

My witch jumped, dropping Sin's hand like she hadn't even known that she'd been holding it.

She shrugged, sheepishly. "Sorry."

"*Forgiveness can be bought with strokes,*" I offered, magnanimously.

For the Great Satan was a forgiving Satan.

My witch plucked me up, holding me to her chest. Her lavender scent instantly surrounded me against the stench of the cemetery. I was always safe at her side or snuggled against her.

She scratched behind my ear. "So, no autopsies, necromancy, or digging up bodies...and I'd thought that today was going to be fun. What next?"

"What a shame. Especially since this charming young witch looks like a real adventurer," a dashing voice drawled from the shadows of the cemetery. "Not at all like most of the dried-up prunes, who are constantly summoning me."

I startled, and my hackles rose, as a ghost materialized in front of me.

The ghost was a rakish Victorian in a crimson suit that was threaded with gold. His hair flamed red, and his eyes were as emerald as mine.

If I hadn't already decided on the dragon...*and he*

*hadn't been dead...*the ghost would've made a hand-some mate.

Plus, he was a mage, and witches and mages had been at war with each other for ages.

Although my witch didn't care about that kind of nonsense. It was one of the things that I loved about her: war blindness.

To be fair, it was lucky because witches were at war with pretty much everybody.

On my whiskers, I'd known that Witch Hollow was the most paranormal village in England, but I still hadn't believed that I'd truly see a ghost.

I perked up.

"A g-g-ghost," my witch, stuttered.

"A-at y-your s-s-ervice," the ghost mimicked, before sketching an impressive bow. "I'm Lord William." He mock glared at Sin. "Where have you been? I'm bored out of my mind."

"That's not difficult," Sin muttered.

William stuck his nose in the air, pretending not to hear him. "Why haven't you been around lately, Sinclair? The village has been the poorer for it. Such riff raff nowadays. No class at all."

"Hold up." My witch clasped Sin by the arm, drag-ging him away from William, who watched with inter-est. "Why are you just chatting with a...?"

"*Snob spook?*" I suggested.

She shivered.

My witch was scared.

The veils between life and death could be crossed, and sometimes, they touched. Yet the connection was sacred. Whatever was occurring here in the village wasn't natural.

Perhaps, I should help my witch overcome her fear of spooks.

When I'd first been created and hadn't known that witches were forbidden from contacting the dead or summoning them (they mustn't have seen the memo in Witch Hollow), I'd been terrified that ghost familiars were haunting me.

Lay off, it was chilling.

Would this help my witch?

Satan's Step-by-step Guide to Overcome Your Fear of Ghosts

1. Remember they're not chickens. Nothing is as scary as chickens.

2. What's the worst possible outcome if you confront a ghost? Aye, it could kill you, but... *Possibly best to skip this step.*

3. Remember, it's more scared of you, than you're scared of it. *Probably.*

4. If it was good in life, then it'll be good in death. You only have to worry if it was a wicked witch, psycho, or serial killer... *Possibly best to skip this step too.*

5. Imagine the ghost naked. Try it.

My witch sneaked a glance at William, who winked. "I'm the poster child for breaking the rules, but the only way that a ghost could be here is if..."

"Mediums and witches ignored the rules and messed with the natural laws around the dead...?" Sin inspected his fingernails, as if checking them for lingering dirt. "I'm aware that witches aren't meant to study the dead, but the paranormals in this village are all..." His mouth twisted like he was searching for the polite word, "...*rebels*. Their combined powers make the ghosts visible and *pests*. William's harmless. He's just lonely."

"Oh, I wouldn't say that I was *that* harmless." William's legs melted to mists, and he floated towards us.

I liked him.

"*Look*," I urged my witch, "*just remember that he's not a chicken or was it, imagine that he's a naked chicken...?*"

Sin ducked his head. "Don't catch his eye, don't catch..."

"Too late," William singsonged

"Attention whore," Sin muttered.

William grinned, unapologetically.

A cold breeze blew around us, bristling my fur, as William wound around us like we were bright trinkets for him to examine.

It must be boring stuck in the cemetery.

Did he not have someone like I had my witch? Was he claimed by anyone?

I tilted my head. "*Can you hear me?*"

William brushed his hand over the air above my ears, and it was like being nipped by ice.

I narrowed my eyes, and he laughed, pulling away his hand.

"I certainly can hear you, sweet kitten. Cats are most closely attuned to ghosts, and so more haunted than any other animal." *I knew it.* I forced myself to arch toward him, rather than away. His eyes widened, and then he stroked his hand over me with a surprised smile. "Well, aren't you quite the delight. I shall make a concerted effort not to frighten you off but I can't speak for this strapping dragon here because he has rather a large fire problem."

Sin crossed his arms. "Not a problem, more of an *issue*."

My witch narrowed her eyes. "So, William here is a good guy. But how many ghosts are we talking?"

Sin and William exchanged a glance.

William raised his brow. "Madam, don't alarm yourself, but there are many generations of ghosts here. If it helps, most choose to be dwellers of darkness."

Could he have made that sound any more sinister (unless he'd thrown in a laugh of doom)?

My witch nudged Sin. "Remind me not to accept

any offers of romantic midnight strolls." Then she marched to the edge of the cemetery, studying the village green beyond. "Why isn't this place teeming with reapers?"

William shuddered, hiding behind Sin like the Sheriff would protect him.

Sin rolled his eyes.

On my whiskers, my witch needed to attend a How to Talk to the Deceased Seminar.

"Reapers have an agreement not to reap in certain places, including Witch Hollow." Sin prowled to my witch's shoulder. "Ghosts aren't dangerous. They're just caught in this loop of their own pasts. They eternally crave. It's..."

"Agony," William said, softly.

When he ducked his head, fiddling with the buttons on his waistcoat, his red hair tumbled over his eyes.

Get on with you, a demon familiar could wish to snuggle a sad ghost.

Sin's smile was equally sad. Why would the claimed shifter look like that? Here's the thing, he might not know that he was claimed yet but a *hair on trousers claim* was strong.

I'd bet my tail that Sin didn't break it.

"Eternally craving for your past...or someone...that's hard." Sin shrugged. "It's what anchors ghosts to this world. Sometimes, it's a craving for redemption, revenge, understanding...or a friend. It varies." He turned to eye William. "I've always wondered if this one craves someone to bore."

William's lips quirked, before he hurriedly hid his smile. "I demand satisfaction, Sinclair! If I could hold them, it'd be pistols at dawn!"

"You'll have to satisfy yourself with a death glare, instead." Sin chuckled.

My witch studied Sin. "You two are mates."

Sin and William both froze.

"Absolutely not," Sin spluttered.

"The very idea." William sniffed.

"*Best pals*." I clapped my paws together. "*Just an average dragon and ghost bromance*."

My witch smiled. "Willy here's just like I imagined your mate would be."

"Willy?" William gasped, outraged,

Sin smirked. "So, Willy, have you heard any gossip about a murder?"

William sulkily floated over to a gravestone and settled on top of it. "You know that the other ghosts never stop talking about their own murders, or their relatives' murders, or who they *want* to murder..."

"Inspector Lanira Marchbanks was killed yesterday," Sin explained.

William's eyes lit with a glee that I recognized as just like my own diabolical joy in something...like when I'd gained control of England's human weapon

budget and swapped it with the aid one. *Allegedly.*
"What a terrible pity. That's fake regret and grief, by
the way, to stop myself dancing a jig. The old bat was
pushing for the Council to review the mediums and
witches who break through the veils. Most of them are
annoying, but if they'd been banned, then what
would've happened to us ghosts?"

His expression became stricken.

Could you die if you were already dead? James
Bond could die twice, but it wouldn't be fair for the
ghosts.

Marchbanks had been hated by both the living and
the dead. That was impressive.

Since she'd been trying to wipe so many of them
out, control, or shut them down, then it wasn't
surprising.

My witch cradled me closer.

"Okay, let's add mediums and ghosts to the not so
short list." My witch squinted through the light at the
village green.

"Shall we?" Sin gestured like he was inviting my
witch and me to a ball and not into a village that had
banned him for burning it.

I clawed my way to my witch's shoulder, waving
goodbye to William, who faded back into the
shadows.

I missed the sad ghost already.

Could demon familiars keep pets? I could convince my witch that ghosts were an acceptable pet.

Why did facing the bright sunshine of Witch Hollow make my fur bristle with fear, more than the dark of the cemetery? Which suspect would we meet first and what danger?

CHAPTER EIGHT

Hollow Green, Witch Hollow

ASTRA

I strolled away from the cemetery and into the village green of Witch Hollow with Sin following me closely behind like I wasn't still shaken by my first ghostly encounter.

Okay, Lord Williams had been more like the annoying cousin who corners you at a wedding than the malicious spirit that Morgan had warned me about. She'd told me that witches were forbidden from communing with the dead because then the dead would have too much power over the living.

But who was I to be judgey, if Sin wanted to be

the Crazy Ghost Earl, when I was already the Crazy Familiar Lady?

Why was Sin more relaxed with William, than he was with me?

Hollow Green was huge but as neat as Silver Hall. The grass looked like it'd been clipped with nail scissors. I grimaced, remembering the way that Marchbanks had measured my sign. I'd bet that it had been. *Perhaps, by pixies.*

I narrowed my eyes against the sun, studying the duckpond in the center, which was ringed by bobbing daffodils. At least Marchbanks hadn't stamped on these ones.

The houses and shops, which faced onto the green, weren't uniform and cardboard cut-out, as I'd expected like the whole village had been dropped out of a kid's playbox.

Could houses be rebels?

Each one was different but beautiful in its own way. Unique and characterful.

I itched to discover who lived in each one.

As I watched, an Unseelie fae with golden wings stalked out of an emerald building on the corner. He was arm in arm with a curly blue-haired Light Elf.

I vaguely recognized them from the opening but I'd been too busy then to take much notice.

They strolled together around the square, before turning off down an alley further into the village. I longed to follow them, which was weird because I didn't normally have the time or interest to care about other paranormals.

Sin glanced back at me and grinned. "It's quite a place. When I first came here, I…" He broke off, and his fists clenched. "Can you feel the spells woven into the air?"

"*Burn my whiskers and call me a dog,*" Satan gasped. "*If someone were to harness this power they could…*" I raised my eyebrow at him. "*…help familiars and other good, nice, non-suspicious things.*"

"The magic belongs to the village," Sin said with a hint of steel that I hadn't heard before, and was both thrilling and hot. Perhaps, he was better at being Sheriff than he thought. "No one steals it."

"*Stealing's a flexible word.*" Satan rubbed his head against my cheek. "*Just like belonging.*"

"It really isn't." I tapped his nose.

Satan pouted. "*Fine. You'll never prove that I stole the village's magic.*"

"I never proved that you stole the Queen of the Fae's swan tiara, but it turned up on my pillow."

Satan snickered. "*Away with you, it was your birthday gift. And you look much more beautiful in it than she ever did.*"

I blushed, pushing back my hair self-consciously.

I sneaked a glance at Sin who was sneaking one at me.

Sin coughed. "I'll pretend that I didn't hear that."

Satan nodded. "*That'd be wise*."

All of a sudden, the air tinted to blue. It sparkled, scented with violets. I grinned, holding my hand up to waft it through the sunbeams that were dancing as if with sapphires.

"If the village likes and accepts someone," Sin explained, "then it adapts to honor them. As I said, spells woven into its very fabric." He wet his dry lips, before asking, "Blue's your favorite color then?"

I nodded, still wiggling my fingers through the light. Satan purred, waggling his paw to mimic mine. Blue was also his favorite color.

Was the village welcoming me, him, or *both* of us?

"What color did it turn for you?" I asked.

Sin's expression shuttered. "It didn't."

He abruptly turned away, prowling around the pond.

I had to half-run to keep up with him, curling my hand around Satan to keep his furry body on my shoulder.

Why did Sin have such long legs? Although, I didn't mind that they ended in such an enticingly tight…

I hurriedly looked away.

I needed to wear a magical No Romance Ring. They were like chastity rings, but instead, when you thought of men romantically, they filled your mind with hideous images of your most embarrassing romantic moments: like the time that you kissed someone without realizing that you had something in your teeth or started dirty dancing with your partner at a party, only to realize that you'd mistaken them in the dark and were rubbing yourself against a complete stranger…

Not that any of those humiliating moments had happened to me. *Of course.*

It was drastic, but at least then I'd stop tingling every time that I looked at a certain dragon shifter.

Except, the ring would make it a little hard for me to finish reading *Pride and Prejudice.*

"*Why don't you just bite his arse and then pin him down?*" Satan suggested in a seductive purr.

Sin's shoulders stiffened.

Sometimes, having Satan on my shoulder truly was like…*having Satan on my shoulder.*

"Remind me not to show you any more wildlife documentaries." I glanced at Sin, who'd stopped at a twisted oak bench that looked as ancient as the village.

It was also scorched and blackened.

Okay, now I believed the whole *scorching the village bench incident.* But this was a wealthy village who loved everything to look perfect. Why hadn't they simply thrown this old one out and replaced it?

And why had it been such a serious offense to damage it?

Silver dragons were known for their tempers. If this was the worst that he'd done, then Sin was practically a pacifist.

"What's your favorite color then?" I asked on impulse.

Sin's shoulders relaxed, and he traced his finger along the back of the bench. "Silver. But I'm becoming partial to blue."

When his intent gaze met mine, I pinked.

Where was the No Romance Ring when I needed it?

When the ducks floated closer to the edge of the pond, *quacking* at Satan, he hissed. I petted his back.

"They're not chickens," I soothed. "This is a Chicken Free zone."

"*Ducks are the chickens' family.*" Satan's eyes narrowed. "*I don't trust poultry allies.*"

Sin snorted. "While your familiar wages war against the village ducks, why don't we decide who we visit first on the short list?"

"I just don't get how one person can be so hated. Yeah, she was a pencil-pushing, narrow-minded, officious… Okay, I'm stopping before I answer my own question. But I mean, by *so* many people? Was it just that she ran the Witch Inspectorate?"

Sin shook his head. "Not that she ran it. That she

took *delight* in it. Look around you. This village was created for those who are different. It's meant to be about tolerance."

"*Pull the other one that has witch's bells on*," Satan muttered.

Sin traced his finger along words that'd been carved into the bench.

Was it a dedication?

It still bothered me why such a visible symbol of Sin's crime had been left in the center of the village.

A Home for All in Need for A Night or Forever

I wrinkled my nose. "Wow, how generous to offer a wooden bench to the homeless."

"*Witch Hollow*," Sin corrected, haughtily. "That's the motto of the ten founding families. Their descendants, the Founders, still run this village. The Inspectorate, Council, boards, and the Mayor…they've always had the power. And Marchbanks is one of those ten families."

I drew in a sharp breath. "She was a Founder?"

"*Always take off the head of the snake*," Satan said, approvingly. Then with a slow, innocent blink. "*I'd imagine*."

I fixed him with a hard stare. "You know, this whole *prove my demon familiar innocent* campaign of ours would go a whole lot better if you acted innocent."

Satan only cackled like he was *totally* guilty.

I ran my fingers over the cracked word; its magic smarted across my skin. "I get now why they went so crazy about the whole burning their founding bench. Yet you must know that they also need you, Sin. They can't blame you when you have a loss of flame control, but then turn to you to solve their crimes. It's not fair." Sin's eyes were wide, and he studied me like he'd never seen me before or like he'd never heard anyone stick up for him. That made my chest tight with an emotion that I wasn't ready to examine yet. "You're not feeling any flame issues now, right?"

He glanced at the bench; his lips thinned. His magic wove out of him in silvery waves.

Then he held up his finger. "Just give me a minute." He took a deep breath, before letting it out. "By my wings, the bench is just so damn tempting. Such a fine piece of wood, and the flames when it went up were glorious."

I eyed him. "Are all dragons…?"

"Just me."

"Good to know." I edged around the bench, resting my hand on his elbow.

Instantly, Sin's breaths became less ragged.

He shot me a small smile. "Look at that. You can tame a dragon."

How many times could I be embarrassed in one morning?

I'd better not go for the record because I was really, *really* good at embarrassing myself.

My expression softened, and I didn't pull away my hand. "Do you live in that big mansion all alone? Well, apart from your psycho butler."

Sin let out a surprised huff of laughter. "A lot of us live alone here in the village. Before Granddad died, I worked in the Silver Court of Dragons, alongside my brothers and sisters. That was more…" His hand fell to the hilt of his sword. "…you know, *fight*, deadly wars, *fight*, rivalry, *fight*, and…" He cut off, before tucking a stray strand of my hair behind my ear like he didn't even know he was doing it. "Now, I'm more into checking the height of my hedges and attending book clubs."

I brightened. "There's a village book club?"

Sin grinned. "A magical one, which has quite the twist in the tale." Then he shrugged. "Perhaps, I've become too stuck in my routines."

"That's me, good at unsticking things."

"*Fine as it is to watch your mating rituals,*" Satan pointed with his paw across the green, "*but isn't that the caterers from our event?*"

I stared at the building, which was rustic with a leather awning almost like it'd grown out of a tree and then been dressed in a fraying skirt.

Yet despite that, the shop held a predatory edge, which was surprising in a bakery, although less surprising in one that was named in bone-white letters:

WILD CUPCAKES

"Why are they wild?" I blurted. "What's a tame cupcake anyway?"

"It's a magical bakery run by wolf shifters from the Kingdom of the Wilds." Sin pulled away from me, marching towards the shop. "A brother and sister. They're on my shortlist, but it won't be them."

"Why?"

Sin's gaze became flinty. "We're only talking to them to prove that we can cross them off our list."

"Just like we're doing for *my* familiar?" I demanded.

Sin nodded. *It wasn't convincing.*

When Sin ducked across the road, I followed him. My pulse thudded.

What would I discover in an enchanted bakery run by werewolves?

CHAPTER NINE

Wild Cupcakes Bakery, Witch Hollow

ASTRA

When I pushed into the bakery, *Wild Cupcakes*, followed by Sin, and the bell above the door *tinkled* merrily, I forced on a polite smile, even though my heart beat too rapidly in my chest.

Witches had defeated the werewolves in the Wolf War, and until recently had taken their Omegas hostage as slaves in all but name as a way of keeping the peace. Omegas were always male, just as Alphas who ruled in their kingdoms were female.

Morgan had been too busy building our demon familiar empire to want to keep a werewolf around.

So, on top of freeing my own familiar, I hadn't needed to fight for a wolf's freedom. I'd have been devastated to own a shifter.

I even squirmed with guilt, when I discovered a lipstick that I hadn't worn for months, as if I'd ignored an old friend. It was why I'd developed a rotation system, so that none of them would feel left out.

I might've developed a guilt complex.

I wasn't the same as most of my witch friends, and I definitely wasn't the Omega owning type.

Yet the wolf shifters who owned this bakery didn't know that about me. For all they knew, I cruelly wore down my lipsticks, until they were uneven on one side and fluffy and then abandoned them at the back of cold, dark drawers.

You know, *that* kind of wicked witch.

A werewolf had as much reason to murder a witch as anyone.

With that reassuring thought, I glanced over my shoulder at Sin, who rested his warm hand on my lower back. I let myself be guided further into the bakery.

It had nothing to do with the delicious shiver that his touch sent through me.

Of course.

Eels' "Lone Wolf"'s eerie rock blasted through the bakery.

Perfect. A werewolf with a sense of irony.

Satan swayed on my shoulder to the music. "*This is more like it. Even if they're guilty, we're letting them off, right?*"

I arched my brow. "Simply because they've got an epic taste in music…?"

"*It's the best defense.*"

I rolled my eyes.

It always helped to be reminded why it was a good thing that demon familiars didn't rule the world.

Defense by musical taste: M'lord she was caught listening to the Glee *soundtrack on repeat.*

Verdict: *Guilty.*

I gazed around the bakery in astonishment. It was like stepping inside a forest. The ceiling was dappled green, and the walls twisted like tree trunks. I bounced up and down on the floor, which was springy with moss. Mouth-watering aromas of chocolate and pastries wound around me in a delicious embrace.

"*Do you need a bib? You're drooling.*" Satan snickered.

I wiped my mouth, before I could stop myself.

"I'd been planning to buy you something but I guess you don't want it then," I replied.

"*Cruel,*" Satan sulked.

We were the only customers, and the bell announcing our entry had been drowned out by the music.

I took the opportunity to glance at the counter.

Tempting cakes, buns, and cupcakes rested on glossy tree trunks that were spun out of sugar. They glittered and sparkled with magic.

I was definitely buying something...*as long as these werewolf bakers weren't the killers.*

A buttery blond-haired Omega, who was dressed in a crisp white suit with an apron over it that made him look adorable, danced to the music, as he pulled a fresh batch of cupcakes out of the oven.

It was the same werewolf who'd delivered a single cupcake to me. I'd been pretty out of it at the time because I'd collapsed in exhaustion, having overdone my renovations on Evermore Farm. But I'd bet my broomstick that Satan had summoned him by Dark Magic.

That didn't mean that I could prove it.

Satan had been in charge of arranging much of the opening, including the caterers.

Why did that no longer feel like it'd been a good idea?

The Omega wiggled his ass, punching the air and singing along to the lyrics with a musical Scottish voice.

Chocolate smeared his soft cheek.

Okay, now I was regretting not having a werewolf. Except for the whole *slave* part. But a cute guy who cooked cupcakes, wiggled his ass, and sang would've been great.

When I caught Sin's gaze, he shot me a disgruntled glare.

Perhaps, he was worried that I preferred someone else's ass to his?

"Don't worry, I won't bite his ass and pin him down. If I intend to do that to anyone, it'll be you." I patted Sin's arm.

The Omega paled, finally noticing us. He dropped the tray with a clatter, and the cupcakes rolled across the floor.

I winced. *Whoops...*

So much for not acting like a typical witch.

I wasn't much of a body language expert. But the Omega's behavior screamed guilty of something.

"*Stop scaring the wolf.*" Satan rubbed his cheek against mine.

Okay, perhaps screamed terrified.

The Omega cringed against the back wall.

His golden eyes with sinfully long eyelashes, however, flashed. "Nay, I won't go back. You can't make me."

I blinked. "Good because I have no idea what you're talking about."

"Woolsey, do my teeth need to take a trip to your backside? On fear of silver, that's the second tray that you've dropped today. How about less dancing and more baking?" An Alpha bustled out the backroom, as if into a battle.

The Alpha was dressed in a layered leather dress, which was frayed until it appeared like fur and dyed red, as if it'd been soaked in blood. Bracelets of fangs encircled her wrists, just as fangs were used like combs to pin back her shoulder length hair. Green warpaint streaked her forehead.

It was startlingly in contrast to her brother: a warrior to his baker.

Woolsey wet his dry lips. "Sorry, Gara. Goddess Moon, are we in trouble?"

Gara turned in surprise to scrutinize me, before her eyes narrowed. Then she stepped protectively in front of her brother.

I hated feeling like the bad guy. Weren't we meant to be the intrepid detectives finding out the truth?

What'd gone wrong?

"We want to prove your innocence," Sin soothed.

Did we?

Gara's shoulders relaxed. "Aye, but we answered your questions yesterday. We catered the event but that's it."

Sin sauntered forward to lean on the wooden counter. "You won't be able to trade properly, while this murder is hanging over your head. Everybody knows that you supplied the food."

Gara's fangs lengthened, and I froze. "Will you tell me something that I don't know? Are you just here to protect your investment then?"

Sin held out his hand, and Woolsey shyly slipped around his sister to take it. "Of course. I invested in both of you, as much as this business. I needed to be certain that you're both all right and don't need anything from me."

Gara's expression softened. "We'll be fine when you sort this out."

"He will," Woolsey said with a trusting certainty that shook me.

"*The shifter has a cheerleader*," Satan purred.

"So, *you* own this bakery?" I demanded.

Sin ran his finger though a lemon cake's icing, before sucking on it; I flushed hot and cold at the sight. "I bought it for Gara and Woolsey because they needed it, that's all."

"And you didn't think that it was a conflict of interest?"

Sin shrugged. "Everybody knows everybody in this village and has done, often for generations. There's always a conflict of interest."

"But why..." I studied the werewolves, who studied me back, warily. "Why would you decide that an Omega baker was an ideal opportunity?"

Gara slammed her fist down on the counter, and I jumped. "Don't call him *Omega* like he has no right to a real name. In this village he has a name: it's Woolsey."

I flushed. "Sorry, Woolsey."

Woolsey shot me a sunny smile, before edging forward. "I'm adding you to my friends list. Most witches in this village still call me Omega, including Marchbanks. My sister refuses to serve those idiots"

"We ran," Gara said, softly. "My brother would've been sent to an Omega Training Center, where he'd have been hurt and then chosen by a witch. By my fangs, I wouldn't let that happen. We wore collars that made escape from the Kingdom of the Wilds impossible. But there were resistance fighters amongst the witches, mages, and vampires. They helped us hide, until all wolves were freed by a witch called the Wolf Charmer. After that, we ended up here."

"Moon knows, we had nothing but the clothes on our backs." Woolsey nuzzled against his sister for comfort. She stroked his hair, and he whined, rubbing his head against her neck. Now he definitely reminded me of my familiars. "Sin found us sleeping on the bench on one of his patrols."

"Aye, we thought that he'd burn us." Gara's lips quirked. "Instead, he offered to buy us a business to run."

Sin clasped his hands behind his back, uncomfortable. "You do understand that you're entirely destroying my bad boy image…?"

"*Away with you, more like a cuddly dragon image.*" Satan smirked

Sin had helped the destitute werewolves to settle

in the village. But more than that, he'd invested in them. He acted the cold recluse but in truth, he befriended lonely ghosts and helped out penniless shifters.

He was a good man beneath the dragony bluster.

Why did he hide it?

Weren't dragons from the Silver Court meant to act like that? Just like I wasn't meant to care about magical familiars?

Was he secretly helping this village in the true spirit of the Founders in the way that their descendants no longer were, to offer those who needed it a home?

Kind of like I was offering shelter to the familiars?

It might be a crazy notion, but maybe we could help each other, as soon as I proved that Satan was innocent, and Sin proved the same for his friends.

Satan jumped off my shoulder onto the counter. He sauntered to a striped pink bun, taking a long lick with his little pink tongue. Then he shot me a smug look.

Now I'd have to buy it.

Sneaky.

If I licked Sin would that make him mine as well?

"*I'm just being your official taster like they used to have ages ago in the covens.*" Satan winked. "*If I turn green or explode into feathers, then you'll know that it's not safe.*"

"But you'll be green or a feather explosion," I protested.

"*See what I'm prepared to sacrifice*?" Satan said, nobly, taking a second lick.

"Why don't you just eat it yourself as a reward for your bravery?"

"*Such kindness.*" Satan nibbled the bun. "*It's like I've died and gone to demon...obviously not heaven but back to the underworld and that's a fine thing.*"

I caught Woolsey's eye; I'd forgotten that the were-wolves couldn't hear Satan. "I'll pay for that. He says that it's the best thing that he's put in his mouth."

Okay, could I bite off my own tongue?

Sin chuckled, but Woolsey's smile was radiant.

Were all shifters gorgeous?

Woolsey pushed a cupcake towards me that was still hot. Gooey chocolate oozed in its center like an erupting volcano. It must've been part of the same batch as the ruined ones, which still lay abandoned and forgotten on the floor.

"On the house," Woolsey offered.

I took a second to mourn the lost cupcakes, feeling that same twinge of guilt that I usually experienced for my forgotten lipsticks.

Perhaps, Zosia was right that I was oversensitive?

When I bit into the cupcake it was like a volcano truly had erupted. Flavors hit me in a sudden wave and each one triggered an emotion: chocolate brownies that Zosia used to make, gingerbread shared with Satan on our first Christmas Eve together, and cinnamon flavored hot chocolate that I'd drunk cuddled with Starlight.

I gaped, closing my eyes at the onslaught.

It was overwhelming.

Then I carefully opened my eyes again and stared at Woolsey. "What was that?"

Woolsey beamed. "My latest invention: The Memory Cupcakes. It takes special memories and binds them into the flavors."

"*Enchanted bakery*," Satan reminded me. "*Can we keep the lad? He has skill.*"

Yet if the wolves had magic, then they'd have been able to hex Marchbanks.

"Who casts the spells?" I asked.

"An Unseelie fae who lives in the village. The Fae are well known for their enchantments and feasts." Gara crossed her arms. "Is this the interrogation now, Sheriff?"

She looked pointedly at Sin.

Sin smirked. "I wouldn't dare with you. Anyway, I know as well as you do that you don't know magic. You bake and invent the creations but you don't cast them."

"Then why are they on your short list?" I demanded.

Gara's nails lengthened to golden claws, which she

rapped on the counter in a way that sent shivers trooping down my spine.

Sin pointed around at the forest interior of the bakery. "Because I checked, and Marchbanks threatened to close this place twelve times."

Gara stiffened. "Aye, but she never succeeded, did she?"

Woolsey stroked Satan, and Satan purred, arching happily into the petting. "Right, like she would ever have stopped trying. On my fur, she couldn't abide shifters, and especially that an Omega was living as an equal to an Alpha."

"*Ask them what else she couldn't abide*." All of a sudden, Satan's ears twitched with interest.

"We know that everybody hated Marchbanks," I said. "But my kitten has just made a great point."

"*Of course*," Satan muttered.

"Who did *she* hate? Who was she closest to closing down?"

"Apart from you?" Sin deadpanned.

I clenched my jaw. "Obviously."

Woolsey rocked back on his heels in excitement. "Edel!" He looked at me like this should mean something, then wiped his hands down his apron and explained, "Marchbanks' sister. She runs a florists and sells magical plants."

"Dangerous plants," Gara added.

"Marchbanks planned to shut it down. What kind

of rotten sister would do that?" Woolsey leaned against his sister, and she wrapped her arm around him.

For the first time, I regretted not having a sibling.

Sin's brow furrowed. "Why haven't I heard about this? I don't even have her down on—"

"Your wee short list?" Gara's lips quirked. "No need to feel inadequate. It's off the books, so far. But us small business owners talk, and Marchbanks threatened her sister, who's one powerful witch."

It hung in the air between us that it'd take a paranormal with powerful magic to burn a witch to ash.

If Edel, who hadn't been at the opening, had somehow managed it from a distance, then she was seriously powerful.

Okay, witch with almost no power wasn't worried at all…

Satan butted me with his head. "*The Great Satan shall protect you.*"

I smiled because he always had, unless it came to chickens. Then he ran.

Gara gave Sin a long look. "We didn't see you at book club last night."

He snorted. "The murder killed the mood for me."

"Will you bring your *lady friend* next time?"

"I inherited her," Sin blurted.

The shifters nodded like this explained everything.

"There was a mouse familiar at the opening."

Woolsey's gaze darted to mine and then away. "He glowed all these beautiful colors."

I perked up. "Rainbow! He's cheeky but one of my favorites. Wait, pretend you didn't hear that. I'm not meant to have favorites or is that only for kids…? He's also obsessed with whittling figures from his favorite fantasy movies. He's currently gnawing with his teeth the entire cast of *Lord of the Rings*."

Woolsey's smile widened. "He told me about his Gandalf. I promised to spin a beard out of sugar. Fur and fangs, I've always wanted company while I bake because it gets lonely early in the mornings. Could I come and see Rainbow to get to know him?"

My eyes widened, and Satan wound closer to me with an excited *meow*.

Was this *the moment…?*

My first adoption?

"How about if you didn't kill Marchbanks, then I'll set it up?"

Okay, that wasn't the *moment* that I'd dreamed about, but I'd take it.

Yet if the werewolves weren't guilty, then who was? The other powerful Marchbanks witch, Edel, her sister? The other Founders or members of the Inspectorate or the businesses that she'd been threatening to shut down?

The mediums or ghosts?

When Sin caught my gaze, his eyes flashed with concern.

I liked the werewolf brother and sister, and I loved Sin. I was more than attached to my own witchy ass.

Now together Sin and I had to save us all, by solving the murder.

CHAPTER TEN

The Savage Star Restaurant, Witch Hollow

ASTRA

I hadn't expected my promise to Zosia that I'd get my claws into the investigation *by any means necessary* to include meeting the silver-eyed dragon shifter for a romantic meal.

Perhaps, I was taking this whole *fake boyfriend* thing too far…?

Sweet Hecate, it didn't mean anything, right?

Sin had only suggested that we meet here to discuss the suspects because he *really* loved their appetizers…

Yeah, and I'd only chosen to wear my second

favorite *pulling* dress, which was blue velvet and knee length, because it was the first thing that I'd snatched out of my closet and *not* because it made my tits look bigger.

Of course, I wasn't wearing my favorite lace dress because it was the one that I'd planned to wear, when Starlight would've turned me into his Blood Lover.

One night, I'd worn that dress, and Starlight had held my hand and promised to make me his *Queen of the Night* forever.

I was no longer the kind of witch, who believed in easy *forevers*.

Sin and I had spent the day going from business to business, crossing off names on his short list.

Anally retentive your name was dragon shifter.

It turned out that because Edel Marchbanks was a Founder just like her sister, even asking her questions, as if Sin suspected her of a crime, was risky.

Plus, Edel would be grieving for her sister…*if she hadn't been the one to turn her to ash.*

So, we'd done due duty…all day…until my feet had ached. Then Sin had suggested meeting here in the evening.

Cauldrons and broomsticks, I was desperate for a foot rub.

I eyed Sin across the restaurant booth.

Slip off one high heel…lift it into his lap beneath

the table...strong hands digging into the arch of my foot...

I bit my lip hard to hold back the groan. Sin cocked his head and studied me.

Okay, no more naughty foot rub fantasies.

I shivered, crossing my arms.

The stars, which blazed in the black ceiling, pulsed like they were in tune with my heartbeat. It was stunningly like I was lying on my bed in Evermore, staring up at the endless constellations. The Savage Star was a magical, elven run restaurant. The walls undulated like a shimmering ice cave, and the floor gleamed with sapphires.

It was spellbinding.

A delicate female elf had shown us to a dark booth right at the back of the restaurant, while a single ball of light like a fallen star floated in place of a candle.

I took a deep breath of the rich, delicious scents, which cocooned me. They promised to taste as mouth-watering as they smelled.

My stomach grumbled impatiently that our meals hadn't arrived yet, and I blushed.

I'd snatched the menu out of Sin's hands, when the curly-haired Light Elf waiter (the same one, who we'd seen with the fae on the village green), had passed it to him first.

Merlin's breath, this modern witch was having none of that misogyny.

Except, then I'd stared blankly at the runes on the menu.

Typical.

Satan would've probably understood them. In fact, most witches with enough juice for Translation Spells could've.

Sadly, not so much this modern witch.

I'd casually passed back the menu to Sin, and his lips had twitched. "You pick. But know that if I like the look of yours better, I'll be eating it."

"Sounds fair."

Now, I wrapped my hands around the stem of my crystal goblet. When I took a sip, I didn't even try to hold back the groan.

The elven wine was an explosion of purity woven with *decadence*: elderflower, blackberries, and *magic*.

The elves weren't even from our realm, but came from across the veil and the Other World. To even see one and share their magic was a privilege.

"How's a star savage anyway?" I blurted.

In my defense, I'd spent a long time with only demon familiars. And it'd been an even longer time, since I'd been taken out to a classy restaurant.

Even if it was only to discuss a murder.

Sin rested his large hands on the top of the table. "Perhaps, it has a biting sense of humor, which is even more sarcastic than Draco's."

"Is that possible?"

Sin chuckled. "Good grief, I hope not."

I glanced around the booth. "Did I break some kind of elven etiquette like calling the waiter *pointy ears* because I have enough self-worth to know that we're not the ugliest customers in here, but the waiter has hidden us right at the back. It's almost like they don't want the other patrons to see us."

Sin drummed his fingers on the table. "They don't. By my wings, can't you imagine the panic? The villagers may think there was another murder, which is why we have to solve this fast because nothing goes back to normal until we do. The problem is that we have to be thorough, before we confront Edel. It's always better if you can avoid a Founder. Of course, the patrons could simply think that I'm here because the elves have broken some kind of restaurant code."

"There's a code?"

He shrugged. "Probably."

Wasn't it his job to know? Was he such a rebel that he didn't care?

Officious Inspectors like Marchbanks had been desperate to punish businesses for the slightest infraction. She'd been even prepared to *invent* them.

All of a sudden, a revelation hit me like a hex.

I leaned closer, stilling Sin's hands between mine. "You're a terrible Sheriff."

Sin's expression flashed with hurt, before it shuttered. "I've been telling you that."

"But you're a good man."

Surprise and then hope flared through Sin's eyes, before he pulled his hands out of mine and took a deep swig of his wine.

On Hecate's name, he should watch out. Didn't he say that he got all *flamey* when he drank? Elven wine was potent or did dragon shifters handle alcohol better than witches?

"Where's the fluff ball?" Sin demanded, abruptly with enough slur for me to know that shifters *were* affected by wine.

Fluff ball?

I wished that Satan had come with me tonight just to see his expression at being called that.

I stifled my giggle in my palm, as Sin glanced underneath the booth, as if Satan would all of a sudden uncurl himself or *pop* into existence.

Instead, Satan was back at the farm, after insisting that familiars knew when not to become a third wheel.

When I'd insisted that it wasn't *that* sort of date, he'd only stared pointedly at my velvet dress and then politely suggested that he spend the evening teaching Precious the useful skill of finding his witch a mate online.

I didn't know what'd disturbed me more: the

thought of dating someone who wasn't Sin, or Precious learning about Tinder.

I'd made a deal with Satan that he wouldn't allow Precious online, if Satan was allowed to practice whatever magic he liked.

I made a lot of deals with Satan. *We both knew who was in charge.*

"Satan couldn't make it tonight." I leaned back in the booth seat. "He had a date with a cauldron."

Sin blinked. "I don't judge. Love is love, after all."

Satan slow dancing with my cauldron…before jumping into it and demanding a white wedding…

I snickered. "He's testing out Fire Spells, and apparently, I distract him. He needs alone time to concentrate."

Sin's eyebrows rose so high that they were lost in his tumble of dark hair. "You left him alone to burn down your tumbledown farm and demon camp…?" Slowed by the wine, he stumbled to his feet, waving around his hands in alarm. "Come on. We must save your other bizarre…wild…familiars."

Rude but also sort of sweet that he cared.

"*Pfft*," I took another careful sip of my wine, "Satan experiments with *way* more dangerous spells." Sin narrowed his eyes at me. "I mean, I trust him and he's powerful. He needs an outlet for his magic, and his private experiments and pranks are just the excuse. Sometimes, I think that he'll explode without them." *Why could I say this to Sin, when I couldn't voice it to my own family?* "I'm like Satan's anchor. I've become good at watching other magical paranormals, rather than being wrapped up in my own magic, and the danger is always how they can control their power."

My throat was tight; I couldn't swallow. I ducked my head, unable to look at Sin.

Why had I admitted all of that?

Sin collapsed back into his seat. "Like me? What are we if we can't control our natures? Am I a *beast*?"

My head shot up.

Sin looked…*devastated.*

He couldn't believe that I thought the same about him as Marchbanks…?

Witching heavens, I'd never acted the same as the other covens or Morgan. But the strongest paranormals, witches included, needed balances and techniques to help themselves control it.

If they didn't…?

"You're powerful," I replied. "I respect both the man and the shifter. I bet you're a glorious dragon."

He gaped at me, before preening. "I must be crazy: A witch complimenting a dragon's shifter side. Of course, my wings are indeed splendid." He hesitated for a moment, before venturing with a gentleness that he hadn't yet shown, "And so that you know, I've been working on control techniques all my life. Yoga works for me. Meditating. And pilates every morning on my back lawn. You're welcome to join me."

A dragon shifter Sheriff who started each day with pilates…?

I bit the inside of my cheek hard.

You. Will. Not. Laugh.

Had he ever shared this with anyone else?

I smiled. "I'm usually busy with the familiars. You know, feeding, petting, mucking out the minotaur… but okay, let's go for it one morning."

When quiet music piped from the walls, I expected it to be some kind of ethereal elven music (flutes, harps, or violins). Instead, Roxette's tumultuous, epic rock "Listen to Your Heart" wailed through the restaurant like announcing the romantic section of the evening.

Lips pucker up now.

Sin and I both froze like socially awkward statues.

Stop it stupidly thudding heart: there will be no listening to you because the last time that I did, you ended up broken.

The image of the last time that I'd seen Starlight broke into my traitorous mind, and tears smarted behind my eyes.

Sin's expression became instantly concerned, and he leaned forward, snatching my hand.

I stared down to where our hands lay clasped in the light of the glowing star.

Romantic dinner, music, light, and his warm fingers stroking mine…

"Is this a date?" I demanded.

Silence.

I peeked up at Sin; his eyes, which were so expressive, met mine.

He didn't let go of my hand.

"Of course, because I always discuss murders on my first dates," he drawled.

My brow furrowed.

Starlight had.

Sin sighed. "That was my attempt to be *savage*, in case you missed it. I admit that it needs work." My eyes widened, as he leaned across the table and gripped me by the chin. "This isn't a date, Astra. Do you imagine that once I take you as mine, you'll ever be in doubt of it? You'll know when the courting begins."

Was that a warning or a threat?

By the way that my skin tingled, and my pulse fluttered in my throat, I hoped that it was warning, threat, and *promise* wrapped into one.

I'd never experienced this war of emotions or sensations on the dates with the humans in the non-magical world: Kevin, Dexter, or Rory.

They'd been more like timing how long they'd talked about their jobs, counted how many times they'd complained about their boss, mentioned their ex, or took out their phones to check messages.

Perhaps, I didn't have the best score rate. But then, most people didn't let their demon familiar set up their profile.

Sin's plush lips curled into a smile. "Unless you want this to be our first song."

My lips twitched in response. "Shut up. Shouldn't that be Taylor Swift's "Lover"?"

Sin reddened.

Point the witch!

"Aren't you cozy, sweethearts?" A sultry voice purred.

I dragged my hand away from Sin's in shock, as a witch sprawled over the table between us. The star light squeaked and backed out of the way in outrage.

The witch was younger than me with violet wavy hair, turned up nose, and a look that was so knowing it made her appear older than me.

"Well, this is definitely not what I ordered," Sin deadpanned.

The witch smirked, running a hand down her tight black dress, crossing her legs, which were encased in purple net stockings. "But I'm such a feast."

Please, let her be the murderer.

Toads and frogs, we could just arrest her, right? For killing the mood, at least.

"Now this must be some kind of violation of the

code." I was clutching at straws but I'd clutch at them until my dying breath, if it removed this witch from our table.

She studied me, amused. "I'm Cora. I'm delighted to meet you. We're all fascinated to learn who's managed to steal the cold heart of our hotblooded Sheriff so quickly."

"*Cora…*" Sin said, warningly, gripping onto the side of the table so hard that his knuckles turned white.

She ignored him. I had the feeling that she did that a lot.

With a lot of people.

Cora smirked. "After all, I *am* Sin's dear, *dear* friend."

"And getting less dear every minute," Sin snarled.

When Cora patted his head like he was a puppy and not a shifter who looked a couple of seconds away from shifting, I snickered.

Cora shot me a grin, before leaning closer to me. "I'm also a dear friend of sweet Lord Williams, and he hasn't stopped going on and on about this blond witch who was dirty but such a delight."

I flushed.

Wow, that was embarrassing.

She eyed me. "You don't look dirty."

"And you don't look like a killer, but I'm going to

guess that you're one of Lord William's medium friends, who Marchbanks was trying to ban."

Cora gasped dramatically. "Why, you've found me out. What an astounding sleuth you are." She held out her wrists to Sin. "Cuff me."

"Certainly not. You'd enjoy it too much," Sin muttered.

Cora lowered her arms, and her eyes twinkled. "You know me too well." Red spread up my neck, and I couldn't help the glare. *Had she dated Sin?* It wasn't like I didn't have my exes. It was just that they weren't sitting on this restaurant table making innuendos and flashing their legs. She rolled her eyes, before patting my cheek. "The Sheriff's virtue is safe. The only thing he knows about me is stories." Then she murmured, "I'm too much witch for him."

"Charming as it always is to see you, Cora," Sin growled, "this is a private dinner."

Cora slipped to her feet, smoothing down her dress. "You could offend a witch. You know, I came over here to tell you some vital information. I've spent hours searching for you. It's ironic that those with magic can mask their locations from each other in this village, especially when I'm only trying to warn you."

Sin sobered, instantly. My breath caught.

Cora's expression became serious.

She bent over the table, and Sin and I leaned closer until our foreheads were touching. "The ghosts love to talk, but they also listen. The Founders are idiots. They want this murder solved straight away. Like always, they think that it doesn't matter if the person arrested is guilty, as long as they have someone to blame. You know, this whole perfect ideal of harmony only works if there's peace. So, if you don't solve the murder by the end of tomorrow, they're shutting down the shelter and slamming the kitten demon familiar in collar and chains."

CHAPTER ELEVEN

Evermore Farm, Witch Hollow

SATAN

I, the Great Satan, was alone in the farm without my witch.

I was free and unleashed.

My witch hadn't risked bringing in a familiarsitter, since the last one mysteriously abandoned me after only an hour, which could've had something to do with the terrifying tango dancing skeletons that'd mysteriously appeared.

I had no idea where they came from, see, no idea at all.

I could protect the rest of the familiars, when my witch wasn't here. It'd been a fine thing when she'd finally understood that, even if I'd needed dayglow skeletons to help me prove it.

I didn't know whether I approved of her going unchaperoned on a date with the shifter.

Lay off, I was a traditional demon familiar. *Sometimes*. Especially, when she'd spent over an hour straightening her hair, deciding which of her wee lipsticks were feeling sad and needed to be worn, and had chosen her second favorite dress.

I could read the signs. *What if she came back carrying a dragon baby in each arm?*

The bed would always be mine. I'd defend it against encroaching babies. *Perhaps, the dayglow skeletons' tango dancing days weren't over…*

I tried out my best supervillain evil cackle.

Brilliant.

The Rolling Stone's "Sympathy for the Devil" rolled through the attic with a primal beat of drums and piano. I wagged my tail and danced, rapping my paws on the pages of the The Secret Diary of the All-Powerful Great Satan in time with the beat.

I thrilled, allowing my magic to roll through me in waves.

Let me introduce my kitten self: *The irony demon.*

Lay off, I'm the Great Satan, remember?

I could sense the savage stars in the sky above, just as my whiskers tingled with the ancient magic of the wild woods that circled the village, and my fur bristled with the power, which lay beneath the City of Oxford.

I shuddered.

Every day, I struggled to hold my magic inside me. It burned, aching to burst out.

World domination sounded about right, but I'd settle for taking over Witch Hollow, making certain that my witch was treated like a queen, and becoming a warrior kitten who'd be able to stop anybody from hurting her or the other familiars in the shelter ever again.

Weirdly, my witch believed in earning her own way in the world.

She'd forbidden me to take over anything. She didn't need to know about the couple of small islands in the Mediterranean, right?

Yet these times when I could experiment in my lovely attic helped. It was my territory, and I'd sprayed in every corner.

Every cat needed his safe space and nap zone.

I glanced happily around the beamed room at the high arched window, oiled floor, and crimson candles, which were lit. Their flames flickered in the dark. The walls throbbed sapphire in time to the beat of the music and my own glowing magic.

My eyes narrowed at my nap zone of blankets.

It was like this, see, a kitten's private nap zone was

sacred. Plus, my knitted cuddle monkey, Hell, was under there, and nobody cuddled him but me.

Yet Lucky was curled, pretending to sleep on top of *my* blankets. At least he hadn't discovered Hell yet. Thank Hecate for small mercies.

I wiggled around in front of the leather-bound The Secret Diary in order to get in a proper glare.

At last, Lucky opened one of his obsidian eyes, which swirled in a disturbing way. "*What?*"

Remember you're the Great Satan...

My tail stiffened. "*That's my nap zone. How about you go sleep somewhere else?*"

Lucky raised his horn like a threat; were all unicorns this freaky? "*Look me in the eyeliner and say that.*"

I froze. "*Ehm, I'll pass.*"

Lucky huffed, satisfied. Then he closed his eyes, and settled to sleep on my poor, poor blankets.

I'd just have to spray on them later.

When Rainbow squeaked with laughter, I shot him a quailing look, but he only squeaked louder.

The mouse familiar perched on the edge of a tiny iron cauldron in the center of the attic. He glowed yellow, which meant that he was happy.

Rainbow's color changed, depending on his emotion, which was a rare power and should've been cherished.

Instead, his witch had rejected him for it.

I'd taken him as my magician's apprentice. Perhaps, because he understood my cheese obsession.

"*Take no mind of the scary unicorn. I'll protect you*." Rainbow's Welsh voice was filled with both laughter but also the kind of boldness that you'd have expected from a rhino and not a mouse. "*What comes next?*"

I wrinkled my nose, taking in the spicy aromas of the Fire Spell that we were weaving. Rainbow had already dropped all of the original ingredients into the spell.

I had one final check, running my paw down The Secret Diary. I purred, as the diary warmed me like an old friend. This was the most magical item in the room and deserved respect.

MY BRILLIANT CHEESE TOASTIE SPELL

Pepper
Chilli
Oil of Abramelin
Snapdragon
Marigold
Holly
Stinging Nettle

Use the Ritual of Mars and the spirit of the sun

My fur bristled in excitement. I had everything ready, doubling the ingredients to make it burn rather than nicely toast, *apart from the final ingredient...*

The shifter with the flowery suit might be frightened of taking on this Founder witch, Edel, but the Great Satan didn't bow before anyone.

Unless someone discovered a Cheese Deity.

I needed to work out how Edel had hexed her sister even from a distance. My Fire Spell could hex a cheese sandwich, which was placed in the same room as me. But could I toast that cheese sandwich, if it lay on a plate in the kitchen?

Just like the innocent sandwich that was lying there right now: my sacrifice to the imaginary Cheese Deity.

What was the extra ingredient that made fire at a distance possible?

I mean I *could* start a fire at any distance but I couldn't control it to one person and then snuff it out as soon as they were ash.

Hexes were all about emotion, see, they straddled the line between love and hate or something with equal strength. You had to mean it.

I could sense it in my whiskers that none of the business owners hated Marchbanks in a personal enough way.

Yet a betrayed sister might.

"*On my ears, do you think that these wolves will*

truly want me then?" Rainbow changed from yellow to frosty blue. When my witch had first brought him to the shelter, he'd remained blue all the time, before I'd been able to coax him into other colors. "*Don't they care about my…?*"

He pushed his pink nose against his fur like he wanted to gnaw it off.

"*Aye, they love it,*" I replied. "*But then you should see the inside of their shop; they have no taste.*"

Rainbow snickered. "*Suck your tail.*"

I stuck out my tongue at him. "*Why don't you suck it instead?*"

He pulled a face. "*Yuck.*"

I laughed. "*The Omega wants you to keep him company as he bakes. You've landed on your fluffy ass and you'll grow fat on it.*" I sighed, dreamily. "*Just don't forget to invite me to visit.*"

Rainbow's eyes narrowed. "*Carry on you, I'm not some kind of kept rodent. I'm Ambition Mouse. I won't become a tamed house mouse.*"

My tail twitched. "*The Omega fought not to be tamed either. You're a fiery, matched pair like…*"

Ginger.

The missing ingredient!

Edel hadn't started and controlled a fire at a distance. I'd been thinking about the spell all wrong. She'd cast a normal fire hex, before the event, but added in a Delaying Spell with ginger, which delayed the effects of fire.

It was the same spell just with its effects delayed until our event.

So, I had no proof. But if Edel *was* the killer, then I now knew how she'd done it.

I'd cast the basic hex several times already on the sandwich but without the ritual. This made the bread more susceptible to hexes. It wouldn't make it go up in flames, but it'd recognize the magic and welcome it.

This should work…

I nodded at the rows of herbs. "*Add ginger.*"

Rainbow gave me a long look, before snatching a ginger shaving (grimacing because it burned even to hold) and preparing to toss it into the cauldron.

I bounced up and down.

This was it.

All of a sudden, Precious trotted into the room like dog royalty, rather than the tiny orange ball of fluff that he was.

Distracted, Rainbow almost teetered and fell into the cauldron.

I hissed, and a candy Love Heart tumbled out of my mouth, which read:

ANGRY CAT

Precious tilted his head and mumbled, "*What's going on?*"

Although it sounded more like *wassgonon* through the *something* clamped in his jaws.

Precious had better not have hunted and caught one of the other familiars, or I'd have to admit that I'd overestimated my ability to do without a familiarsitter.

Then my eyes widened.

By my tail, my cheese sandwich!

"*Drop it, puppy*," I hissed.

Precious sank his teeth more firmly into the bread, and cheese tumbled down the sides.

Nobody made my sandwiches bleed.

Rainbow looked between us with the ginger still between his teeth.

Don't let him drop it…

These were the times that divided the demon kittens from the actual kittens.

I leaped off the lectern, before prowling toward Precious.

Precious backed up. "*Mine*," he growled.

"*Trust me*," I replied, "*this is one explosive sandwich that you don't want. Drop.*"

Rainbow obediently began to open his mouth, and the ginger snagged on his tooth.

"*Not you*," I yowled.

Rainbow froze with his eyes comically large and alarmed.

"*Fair on you, that's a lovely bit of scavenged food. What a great hunter you are*," I praised, and Precious preened. "*But how about a deal?*" The things that I did in the name of magic… "*If you spit it out, then your Play Servant here will help you find even yummier food. Then you can choose the games before bed, right?*"

Precious sniffed, before slowly…*so slowly…* opening his mouth and spitting out the sandwich.

I pounced on it, skidding it away from Precious with my paw.

"*Now*," I hollered at Rainbow.

In turn, Rainbow batted at the ginger with his paw, and it fell into the cauldron.

Bang!

The sandwich disintegrated to smoking ash. Just like Marchbanks had done at the opening.

Precious whined, cringing against the wall. His fur bristled, until he looked even more like a Tribble than normal.

A terrified one.

Even Lucky opened a lazy eye.

Rainbow danced along the lip of the cauldron. "*Success for the Ambition Mouse!*"

I wound around Precious, rubbing my head against him, until his breathing settled. "*Next time I say spit…?*"

Precious nodded. "*Spit.*" Then he whimpered. "*Are you taking back your offer to be my Play Servant this evening, laddy?*"

"*Great Satan never breaks a deal*," I replied, affronted.

Get on with you, I never get *caught* breaking a deal.

I stared at the smoking pile of ash, which proved that Marchbanks could've been walking around with the equivalent of invisible explosives strapped around her middle without even realizing it. The timer had been set to go off at the opening event of the shelter.

But why...?

I tingled with anticipation to meet the witch who'd been clever enough to both invent this and pull it off.

If my witch and the shifter didn't make such a good match (and I could feel it fluffing up my fur, *mates*), I'd be in paw-sized handcuffs for this crime by now. No one would then have been able to prove Edel's guilt.

Except, Edel hadn't bet on *my* magical strength.

Tomorrow, I'd take a trip to Edel's florists, the Magical Blooms, to help catch a powerful witch.

CHAPTER TWELVE

Magical Blooms, Witch Hollow

ASTRA

When I edged into Magical Blooms, Edel's florist shop, at Sin's broad shoulder, I allowed myself to enjoy the caress of his magic that fluttered around him and the security of his height, which shielded me.

I'd never pegged myself as the witch who'd use a Sheriff as a dragony shield before. But then I'd arrived home last night from my...*on Hecate's name don't say date...*evening out with Sin, and Satan's attic had stunk of smoke and magic.

It'd been like Satan's teenage, rebellious *look at*

the dangerous ritualistic magic I can do years all over again.

I'd dashed to scoop Satan up in one hand and Precious in the other, before I'd noticed the tiny pyramid-shaped pile of ash.

"*It was just a matter of adding ginger*," Satan had nodded at the ash proudly, in the same way that I'd guess regular cats presented their owners with the gift of dead mice. "*I claim the Satan Personal Achievement Award of devious spell work. The hex could've been cast in the morning and then delayed like magical terrorism.*"

This morning, I tried to smile and not imagine singed fur and Satan reduced to ash.

I curled my hand around Satan, holding him tight by the back of the neck. His magic coiled around me in turn.

If Edel was powerful enough to cast hexes like that, then it didn't feel my most sensible life choice to confront her (up there with the year that I'd permed my hair).

Except, I'd do anything to clear Satan's name and make certain that my shelter survived.

Yet Satan didn't appear nervous.

Instead, his body was stiff, and his eyes gleamed in full predatory mode.

He was hunting the witch.

Satan caught my eye; he bared his canines. "*Time for the new witch in town to take over Witch Hollow.*"

How many times did I have to remind Satan that *taking over* things wasn't the shelter's mission statement?

Sin glanced over his shoulder at us in shock.

I tapped Satan on the nose. "Try again."

Satan chuckled and tried to pull an innocent face. *"By my tail, I was just overexcited. I mean, let's take down the wicked witch.*"

"You're looking forward to this aren't you?"

"*Maybe.*"

I wiped at the sweat, which dripped down my forehead. The back of my neck was damp, and my dress clung to my curves in a way that I was certain was indecent. The inside of the florists was hot, and the air was moist. Vines climbed up the walls like I'd stepped into a jungle. I peered at my feet, and something skittered between huge feathered ferns.

I yelped and dived to the side.

Satan's claws dug into my shoulder, as he clung on.

There were no windows, and the vast shop was bursting with both small and giant plants. Some of the biggest reached all the way to the high glass roof.

The morning sun speared through the leaves. I scrunched up my nose against the earthy, sweet scent of the intermingling plants, which was intoxicating, like being drugged by flowers.

There was a round counter in one corner of the room, which was laden with vials and oils for sale. But there was no one serving.

Satan glanced at it intently. Perhaps, he was planning his next spell experiments.

This early, there were also no customers.

Where was Edel? Had she found out that we were onto her?

Was the entire shop about to burst into flames?

Let the answer be no…

"Stop," I yelled, and Sin froze with his foot one step over a purple thorned creeper: A fae Sleeping Vine. "Back up. If you take one more step, then you'll collapse, and I'll have my own Sleeping Beauty on my hands. Except, more like Sleeping Handsome. Would you truly go to those lengths to get me to kiss you?"

Sin paled and stumbled backward. He stared around at the flowers with more respect.

"It would've cursed me to sleep?"

"It's a natural fae plant. They use it in sleep charms." I tilted my head. "I thought that you were big on gardening?"

He snorted. "I'm forced into that because I'm bored and stuck by myself in Silver Hall. It's more like pruning hedges, rather than deadly plants."

"*On my whiskers, you've been missing out.*" Satan's tail wagged. "*Is this shop booby trapped?*"

Why did he have to sound so excited about that like Edel had just laid out feathery treats and balls for him to play with, rather than toxic plants?

I glanced around the shop carefully. Amongst pretty flowers in buckets and harmless plants, were the kind just like those that grew wild in the cemetery, which could be used in magical spells, hexes, and potions. In this village with its paranormal creatures and witches, there'd be as much demand for those, as roses to give to your loved one to apologize because you'd forgotten their birthday.

Again.

Not that I was at all bitter that Starlight had forgotten…*twice.*

Not at all.

Yet there were even deadlier plants than the Sleeping Vine that'd been gathered from all the different kingdoms. Each one had properties that were dangerous to the unwary but also had special meaning to the places, which they'd been torn from. Sacred elven saplings or mosses from the Eternal Forest.

Some of the plants were so rare that I didn't recognize them. I'd bet that Satan did. This must be like a fantastic field trip for him.

For the first time, I had sympathy with Marchbanks wanting to close down this business.

"I don't think that it's deliberate," I replied. "At least, not meant to hurt us. Who knew that horticulture could be this exciting?"

"Seriously?" Sin huffed. "Try *dangerous*. And they banned *me* from the village for one little scorched bench…"

My lips twitched. "The *Founder's* bench…"

He waved his hand. "Details."

All of a sudden, there was a startled yelp from the back of the shop.

My eyes widened, and Sin's eyes flashed.

Was Edel barbecuing her next innocent victim, while we chatted? *Were we too late to save them?*

Sin's magic swooped out of his shoulders, and faster than I'd yet seen him move, he half flew over the deadly floor towards a back room, which had been hidden by the curtain of branches.

I hopped over the vines to follow him, while Satan yelled instructions like he was steering a ship, which was not flattering *at all*.

"*Over the branch, right, left, jump*," Satan yelled, nibbling on my ear to get my attention.

Wait, it was more like I was an avatar in a computer game, and that was worse because I sometimes wondered whether Satan saw me as that…or simply as the provider of food.

I'm pretty certain that he thought my title was the Witchy Provider of Yummy Goods.

"*...and through the door.*" Satan bit harder on my ear as if for punctuation.

When I jumped through the open door, grimacing as I burst through the damp branches, I slammed into Sin's back and tumbled onto my ass.

Satan fell off my shoulder and onto his furry ass next to me.

He mewled, sadly.

I rubbed his head in comfort and glared at Sin.

Sin held out his hand to me and pulled me to my feet.

I couldn't help the shiver at the warmth of his skin and the way that his magic tingled against mine.

Then I stared at the Unseelie Fae, who was hanging upside down from the roof of the tiny potting room. He was wearing a gold uniform with a gardening apron that read: **Born to Magical Garden!**

A plant that looked like a Venus Fly Trap with both attitude and scales had wrapped its tendrils around his ankles; the fae swayed, and his wavy emerald hair hung over his face.

His wings beat weakly.

It was the fae who I'd seen walking alongside the elf in Hollow Green yesterday. He looked younger than me and peeked at us with large, startled eyes.

Edel wasn't here, which was both a relief and a worry like when you knew that there was a spider in the room but suddenly, you lost sight of where he'd run to.

Satan always insisted that spider familiars were loyal, but I could never get over the way that they scuttled.

Why was Sin leaning against the door frame and crossing his arms, rather than letting the fae down? Was he finally playing bad cop?

Well, I guessed that it was my turn to play good cop.

I smiled at the fae, and he shot me a tentative smile back.

When I reached forward to help free him, however, Sin and Satan both hissed in a shocked breath at the same time.

"I wouldn't do that if I were you," Sin said with a hint of smugness.

"Because you have a sadism fae kink?" I gasped.

The fae became ashen. "*Woah*, I don't play without negotiation first." His voice was aristocratic but ethereal. "Let's just all be nice to the *feeling slightly vulnerable here* fae."

Satan snickered. "*I like him, and his hair's pretty. Can I have him as a pet?*"

I shot Satan an admonishing look. "No pets."

"Look at this, the gardening failure becomes the guru," Sin smirked. *Was he about to do a victory dance as well?* "It's a Dragon Snare Plant, which has him in its grasp. I don't know much about gardening, but I know my own kingdom. The Dragon Snare draws magic from its user, while you touch it."

My eyes widened, but it was Satan who skittered wildly backward, recoiling.

"*Holy Mary preserve my whiskers,*" Satan muttered. "*I never knew that such evil existed in the world. Don't let it touch me.*"

"Scaredy-cat." Sin rolled his eyes. "You're safe with me here. And it doesn't remove the magic permanently, just for a while after you've touched it with your skin. It could be hours or a few days."

"*You try living without your magic,*" Satan insisted. "*That's cruel.*"

Satan was right.

I glanced at the fae. "Don't worry. We'll help."

He blinked. "Really? This is my fault. I'm always clumsy."

"Less talking; more action." Sin drew his sword. He looked like a true hero with his weapon out (and in no way would I even acknowledge the innuendo in that). The light gleamed off the steel. Then he marched closer to the fae, who struggled wildly, beating his wings like he expected Sin to cut off his head, rather than free him. "Hold still."

"L-look, I d-didn't mean to get all t-tangled up again…" The fae stuttered.

"Don't worry about his grumpy *I'm an elitist jerk* expression," I advised, "that's just his resting dragon face."

"Such a ringing endorsement," Sin said.

The fae held still, however, as Sin slashed the sword through the creepers.

The Dragon Snare Plant screamed.

I winced. Okay, I knew what I *wasn't* buying as my next houseplant.

The fae tumbled to the floor in a flurry of feathers and *owwws*, as silver goo poured out of the sliced plant and onto his head. It plastered down his hair and dripped over his face, until he looked like a mime artist or an alien.

I stumbled away from the disgusting puddle that seeped from the now snarling Dragon Snare.

"Victory to the magic users!" Satan shook his ass in delight.

But the fae gasped for breath, crawling toward Satan like he meant safety.

"I can't feel my magic," he murmured. "It's like dying."

The fae looked so pathetically sad, drawing his knees up as he watched me warily, that I knelt next to him.

I reached out, delicately petting his soft feathers, which hadn't been splattered in goo.

The fae's eyes became dazed, and he snuggled

closer to me.

Sin flushed, shifting from foot to foot like he wanted to rip me away from the fae; were all dragon shifters so possessive? "A fae's feathers are rather sensitive. Intimate." *Intimate?* Absentmindedly, I drew my fingers across his wingtip, and he curled even closer. "Excuse me, I didn't know that you were so forward with strangers. Perhaps, you wish to be inherited by a fae rather than a dragon?"

Why was he sounding hurt? Wait, intimate as in…*intimate?*

I drew back my hand reluctantly because bubble my cauldron, the fae's feathers were soft.

Okay, unintentional naughty touching.

"Sorry." I reddened. The fae's uniform was ripped, and his translucent collarbone looked deliciously lick-able, even if the rest of him was still dripping in plant goo. "And I haven't even bought you dinner."

"I'm cheap; I'd settle for a coffee." The fee batted his eyelashes at me. Was I being chatted up in the middle of a rescue? Sin snarled at the same time as Satan launched himself on my knee like my kitten knight here to defend my virtue. "You had to go and tell her about the wings, Sin. I needed comforting."

So, the bad cop had been *accomplice* all along…?

Did Sin know everyone in this village? At least,

174

all the crazy rogues, delinquents, and… Sweet Hecate, was that why he'd befriended *me*? Did he collect rebels like other people collected stamps or vintage vinyl collections?

I'd known more reclusive party animals.

I stared at Sin. "Another one of your friends like Lord William…?"

"Lord Piper, actually." The fae inclined his head. "If we go for that coffee, then I'll show you all the ways that I'm very much alive and nothing like a ghost."

"*Brilliant. Then your living arse will feel my claws when I comfort you with them.*" Satan slashed his claws through the air. Satan had become as protective about my fake relationship with Sin as he was about me. "*You wicked witch's apprentice.*"

I held him by the scruff of the neck, before he could launch himself at Piper.

"I can hear your familiar," Piper said in surprise. "But I don't have my magic, so I can't be the one accidentally eavesdropping…"

"Satan likes to *let* people hear his insults," I explained. "He hates wasting them."

Piper pointed forlornly at his **Born to Magical Garden** apron. "I'm the Assistant Florist and not *wicked* just…"

"In need of a kick up the behind for endangering

yourself again." Sin glanced around the destruction of the back room, which was spattered with the remains of the Dragon Snare. I grimaced at the sour stench. "You shouldn't be handling plants like this by yourself. Especially since you're the most accident prone fae that I've ever known."

Piper perked up. "Do I get a medal?"

"You can get an enraged demon familiar loosed on you." Sin shot an amused glance at Satan, who was struggling in my arms now. "How strange that the pussy doesn't like you, when you're such a lovable character."

Piper flicked his hair. "You know you can't quit me."

Satan collapsed into my arms with a chuckle. "*I was right first time about the fae. I do like him. But there'll be no coffee drinking, right?*"

"There'll also be no more working alone on toxic plants," Sin warned (and why was a threat so sexy in that rumbling voice of his?). "You promised me after last time that you wouldn't risk it, and if I'd known that your work conditions were like this…" He sighed. "Truly, you're the reason why half the things go wrong in Witch Hollow."

Piper flapped his wing against Satan's knee in retaliation. "It's more like a quarter. Anyway, I didn't have a choice. Edel's at home grieving for her sister, and so I had to mind the shop by myself."

"*Is this* mind *just like I* minded *the roast turkey in the oven and instead, played computer games? You know, so the roast ended up burned to a crisp…?*" Satan (not so innocently) asked.

I eyed the ruins that remained of the back room and the slowly withering Dragon Snare.

Yeah, this was just like that poor turkey dinner.

Piper paled. "Don't tell Edel that I messed up."

Was his voice shaking from fear or panic, as he pushed himself to his knees? Yet I'd be terrified of Edel as well, if she could turn him to ashes as effectively as Satan had our dinner.

I gestured at the huge, dead plant. "Sort of hard to hide."

Piper furrowed his brow in thought. "It needed pruning…?" Then he snatched Sin's sleeve. "Please…"

Uncomfortable, Sin's gaze met mine. "I'd never get you into trouble. You know that I spend half my life getting you out of it." It sounded like me and my familiars. "Where's Edel now? We just need to talk to her about her sister's death. That's all."

"You can't," Piper blurted. "I mean, she's out at a Founder's meeting. She won't even be back until this afternoon."

Sin's gaze caught mine; his lips thinned. "Then we'll visit her at Marchbanks House and interview her later."

Piper's shoulders hunched, and his wings trembled.

Fear. It was unmistakable now.

After lunch, I had to interview the witch who terrified her own assistant to death and could have literally been the death of her own sister.

CHAPTER THIRTEEN

Marchbanks House, Witch Hollow

ASTRA

Marchbanks House didn't look like the house of a killer.

I didn't know what I'd been imagining a killer's house *would* look like. Perhaps, woven out of angel skins with chainsaw motifs and noxious fumes, while banjo music played like in the *Deliverance*.

I shuddered. Well, that was my nightmares sorted for the next month.

Instead, Marchbanks House was an elegant mansion in pink-hued stone that looked like it should be gracing the front of *Stately Homes and Magical Gardens* magazine, rather than hiding a murderer. I'd learned as a kid, however, that the more ancient the lineage of a coven, then the greater the secrets that they hid.

"Why are we here this early?" I whispered. "Piper said that Edel was out at the Founder's meeting, until after lunch."

Satan had insisted in the name of *oppressed workers solidarity* (did he include himself in that? I shivered at the thought of the havoc, if he ever created a Familiars' Union), that we remain and help Piper clean up the backroom. That'd been a gooey mess of an hour, which I'd never get back, but Piper's grateful smile had made the sticky tangles in my hair worth it.

Then Sin had dragged me into a coffee shop like proving some sort of *coffee claim* on me. Was that one of the steps in dragon dating?

After that, however, Sin had led me through Witch Hollow and the surrounding farmland out to March-banks House, rather than waiting until after lunch, as I'd been expecting.

"Then why are you whispering if no one's here?" Sin raised his elegant eyebrow.

My brow furrowed. "Good point, but so is mine. Walking's healthy exercise, but aren't we under time pressure here?"

"*And my wee legs are tired*," Satan protested, collapsing into a patch of marigolds, which he'd been sniffing.

The marigolds' scent was pungent. The flowers nestled in their feathered foliage in fiery bursts of yellow, red, and orange. Holly and violet snapdragons with blooms like tiny dragons' jaws wove between them. Edel must have the same green fingers as Ursula had at Evermore Farm because this garden was enchanted too; plants bloomed from across all the seasons.

Had my great-aunt and Edel been friends?

I wrapped my arms around my middle. I hoped not.

"I carried you. My legs are tired for both of us," I corrected.

"*Must be phantom pains then.*" Satan padded to the oak front door and then pressed his ear to it like he was listening. "*Aye, nobody's home.*"

"The darkened windows give that away." I studied Sin, who played with the hilt of his sword like a guilty schoolboy. "Again, are we visiting just to admire the garden?"

"We're here because Edel isn't. She lives alone, now that her sister's dead."

"Say that again but so that it makes sense."

Sin's smile was slow, wide, and bad in all the right ways. "If she's out, then we get to explore."

Satan's eyes widened with surprised respect, before he bowed his head. "*You've just earned your-*

self demon points. I give you my blessing as a familiar to join our family."

Sin blinked. "*Ehm*, thank you?"

And this was why you didn't work with demon familiars, or it turned out, dragon shifters.

I narrowed my eyes. "Wait, you made Starlight perform three near impossible tasks, which almost got him killed, before you granted him your blessing, but all Sin had to do was break the law?"

Satan waved his paw at me, impatiently. "*And your point is…?*"

I jabbed my finger at Sin. "And what are you: gamekeeper turned poacher? Do they teach breaking and entering to sheriffs?"

Sin waggled his eyebrows, as he crouched in front of the heavy iron lock, before slipping a twisted length of metal into it like carrying around lockpicks was normal. "Not quite. I may (only according to the scurrilous rumors), have learned this in my wilder pre-sheriff days."

I flapped my hands like somehow a chicken impression would stop him. It was only that so far in my life, I'd broken my parents' rules and my coven's (which by witch standards made me quite a rebel), but I'd skirted committing *actual* crimes.

How ironic that I was losing my criminal virginity to a Sheriff.

"What if we take this risk and we're wrong about the chief suspect?" I demanded. "It's not like the *other* suspects aren't suspicious or without a motive. There's that freaky medium, the friendly ghost, or the cute-as-a-button werewolves. It's not that I want any of your friends to be guilty but… Hold on, what about the Founders themselves? With a name like that, they're bound to be up to all sorts of dodgy stuff. They're powerful, ancient, and elite. I bet they're into secret, cabal things like Dan Brown writes about or…"

"You're babbling."

"Nervous habit, especially before I'm about to burgle somewhere."

"*Away with you, don't worry.*" Satan wound around Sin excitedly like they were accomplices on a heist. "*We won't steal anything, so you're only really trespassing.*"

"Oh, perfect. I've only just finished unpacking all the boxes at the farm. Please don't make me pack them up again to move us to prison."

Satan winked at me. "*Would you take it easy? I'd magic the boxes to the cell, anyway.*"

Well, that was my buttocks unclenched then.

Sin snarled, wiggling the lockpick around fiercely like it'd work by his force of will alone. "This is harder than I'd expected."

Satan raised his paw, and a magic glow enveloped

the door. "*There's extra wards woven beneath it. Let me help.*"

The door swung open.

Sin coughed to cover his embarrassment, as he pocketed his lockpick and stood, wiping his hands down his trousers. "Good joint effort."

Satan grinned, bearing his fangs. "*Satan Personal Achievement Award for Breaking and Entering!*"

"Excellent," I replied. "You're one award away from becoming a familiar gangster."

Satan preened.

Sin edged into the shadowy stone hallway. The walls and ceiling were covered in gleaming mirrors. Magic hummed, low and oppressive. Satan prowled at Sin's heel (he'd definitely discovered a new best friend), and I followed behind.

I wrinkled my nose at the aroma of spicy herbs.

Sin pushed open the first door, and I peered over his shoulder at the kitchen inside.

Again, in my imagination, Edel's kitchen would've been scrawled with sigils for Blood Magic, while a naked human sacrifice was bound to the counter with an apple stuffed in his mouth for effect.

Instead, the kitchen was sunny and pretty with marble counters that had no sacrifice on them, but rather a chopping board and herb pots: chili, garlic, and pepper.

It was way tidier than my own. After all, there were no familiars using the drawers as beds.

"So, what are we looking for? Clues?" I asked, mimicking holding a pipe in a Sherlock Holmes impression.

Satan chuckled. "*Weak.*"

Sin raised his eyebrow. "Edel lived with her sister. You grew up in a coven, so you must know how important family is to witches." I grimaced; *yeah, tell me about it.* "But Lanira and Edel were rivals. Both wanted to be the Marchbanks with the authority in Witch Hollow. Lanira used her role in the Inspectorate to try and shut down Edel's business because Edel was the one with the seat on the Council."

"I bet they were fun at parties," I muttered.

Sin huffed. "You have no idea. Perhaps, Edel wanted such a public death at the opening of a new business, which Lanira was trying to shut down, as a warning to the rest of the Inspectors or as the most ironic death possible."

Satan nodded. "*Witches do love irony.*"

When I turned to Sin, I realized how close we were standing to each other in the doorway. His heat washed over me in heady waves, just like his magic. I pushed him against the wall with a sudden burst of instinctive magic, crushing myself against his hard chest. His breath hitched.

I loved the feel of my magic coursing through me. Was it possible that Sin brought it out of me?

"*Can anyone else feel the heat in here?*" Satan hopped onto Sin's foot, wiggling his furry ass.

Sin's lips quirked.

I reached to push a strand of Sin's hair behind his ear, and his smoldering gaze met mine. "Then why have you been avoiding talking to her? What are you not telling me?"

He glanced at my lips, and his tongue darted out to wet his lips. "Edel is a Founder and in Witch Hollow that means you're close to untouchable. The Mayor's ordered me to find the killer but he wants that to be someone expendable like…"

My eyes flashed, dangerously. "Like…?"

Sin swallowed, before pointing at Satan.

Satan hissed and bit Sin's shoe like he wished that it was a far more sensitive part of him; Sin winced. "*I take back your demon points, you familiar hater. The Great Satan is never expendable.*"

Sin's expression became grim. "Savage my shoe all you like, but it doesn't change the fact that you *are* expendable to the Mayor. So am *I*, by the way, just like Woolsey, Lord William, Cora, and Lord Piper…" When he stroked his thumb across the back of my neck, I battled not to melt into the touch. I was still furious, right? "*Just like you.* He'd dance for joy if I picked a random villager's name out of a hat and then had them dragged off. It's what my predecessors have always done, if they can't immediately solve a case. If I don't, then he'll have me punished."

"Then why don't you?" I demanded.

Sin hesitated, biting at his lip.

Sweet Hecate, I wished to sooth his tortured lip with my tongue, but since I had Sin pinned against a wall, and we were only at the *coffee* stage of our fake relationship, that would possibly be too forward.

"I don't because I'm a terrible Sheriff," Sin said, softly. "But I'm a good man."

I smiled, suffused with warmth.

This investigation was no longer simply about saving my own skin and my familiars'. It was also about protecting Sin and proving that the law in Witch Hollow could be different from now on.

Justice could be real, rather than corrupted.

Sin had a chance to be the true Sheriff that this village needed, and Satan and I could help him stand up to the Founders.

"So, let's get some proof then." I eased away from Sin.

Satan licked over the kitten-sized bite marks in Sin's shoe as if in apology and then hopped off onto the stone floor. "*Like the fact that she owns most of the plants for the Fire Spell...?*" His eyes sparkled, as he attempted an impression of Sherlock Holmes and fell on his face. He rubbed his nose, and I laughed. He shot me an affronted look. "*It's elementary, my dear witch. There are marigold, snapdragons, and holly growing at the front door. Plus, I stung my wee paw on a stinging nettle. On my tail, witches who are hex casters always grow their most potent ingredients close to the door.*"

Crack my cauldron, of course.

Zosia, who was a keen potion maker as well as baker, had her own patch of magical ingredients that she grew by her back door. The closer to the house they were, then the easier they were to cull and dry to be used in potions, spells, or hexes.

Mum and I hardly ever did that style of magic because of the business side of the demon familiar empire. It was the only reason that I'd been able to hide my own magical deficiencies for so long, as well as Satan pretending that his power was mine.

Other witches kept their most potent ingredients by the door, however, as well as…

"The herbs in the kitchen." I gasped. "Chili and pepper are part of the Fire Spell."

Sin shook his head. "It's evidence but it's not proof. How many other people in the village have those ingredients, have bought them from Magical Blooms, or picked them from the graveyard? The Founders would say that if Satan can cast the hex, then *he* did it."

"*Familiar prejudice*," Satan hissed. "*Did you miss

the Oil of Abramelin on the counter in Magical Blooms? Fair on them, they were making a fine profit on it. The oil is a ceremonial magic oil blended with aromatic plant materials. It's also the last remaining ingredient needed in a Fire Spell."

I drew in a sharp breath. *This was it.*

Edel was the murderer. But wasn't the evidence all circumstantial?

We needed more.

All of a sudden, a screaming wail exploded from the walls.

I winced, clasping my hands over my ears and falling to my knees in the hallway. Sin crouched protectively over me, and Satan whimpered, crawling as close to me as he could.

"On my wings, what is this damn noise?" Sin hollered.

"The house is protecting itself from intruders," I yelled back; my temples throbbed. "It must be rusty because it wasn't triggered, when we opened the door. Nobody must've ever been stupid enough to break in, apart from us."

"How do we make this witch alarm system turn off?" When the front door slammed shut with an ominous *crack*, Sin's silver magic fluttered around Satan and me as he added more urgently, "Now would be good."

Frogs and toads, we were screwed...

I knew that there was a reason that I didn't break into witches' houses.

"It's an ancient trick to trap intruders."

Sin clenched his jaw. "You're only warning me now?"

Satan let out a burst of magic in desperation, but it only bounced back from the mirrors, repelled by the house's spell.

I clenched my hands. "No one's bothered with this arcane magic for centuries."

"Well, congratulations, you're in Witch Hollow. We bother." Sin staggered against the wall. "Let's treat this as a learning experience."

Then he howled, as he was sucked into the mirror, which hung on the wall.

"*Bring him back, sneaky evil mirror!*" Satan yowled.

I snatched for his tail, but he dived bravely after Sin like he was a miniature dragon, rather than a kitten.

The mirror sucked him into the wall.

"Witching heavens, stop stealing my… my…*mine*." I gritted my teeth, before I threw myself at the same mirror with equal, stupid, courage.

I'd always thought that I'd die to protect Satan. Willingly allowing myself to be dragged into an unknown wicked witch's trap felt worse.

Okay, here went nothing…

The surface of the mirror melted like thick treacle; it slurped at my skin. I shuddered, as it tongued me.

I tumbled through, landing on my ass in a dark cell, which was surrounded by mirrors.

Gasping, I patted myself down. I wasn't burned to ashes. I was alive.

I'd take it as a win.

I was trapped in a really *un*fun funfair ride and alone. But I was alive.

Where was Sin and Satan?

Satan would be freaking out if he was alone.

All of my thoughts were instantly scattered, however, when the mirrors filled with images of my familiars. I reached out, and the tips of my fingers grazed the glass. The familiars lined sadly around me on all sides, but their heads were bowed by heavy collars.

Precious whimpered, raising his scared gaze to meet mine. Lucky lay dejectedly next to Frisky, the griffin. Pumpkin and Spice, the ferret twins, rode on Kid's shoulders, shivering with fear.

Pumpkin and Spice should only ever shiver with naughty anticipation of their next prank.

The familiars were collared, rounded up, and *broken* because of me.

I hadn't kept them safe and now they'd be mistreated again.

I'd failed them.

Tears chased down my cheeks, and a sadness worse than any apart from my deepest "Wrecking Ball" moments washed over me.

My eyes closed.

Why didn't I just sink to my knees and surrender to despair forever? Why didn't I…?

Then my eyes snapped open.

A snarky, loving, and brave familiar called Satan was why. He wasn't collared or broken because he was *real*.

This despair was nothing but a trap.

These lost familiars were nothing but a trap.

Satan, your witch was coming for you.

I gritted my teeth and once more, pushed against one of the mirrors.

Merlin's breath, let this work…

This time, falling through the surface was like being sucked through tar.

I fell through into a dark oubliette with an *oomph*, catching myself with my hands. I sat up, rubbing at my elbows. Many covens had these circular, stone dungeons, where prisoners were trapped to be forgotten.

I'd never checked to see if the House of Demons had its own oubliette, but it was the type of threat that Morgan would've loved to hold over her rivals.

Stop your complaint about the demon familiar you ordered or forever languish in my oubliette.

Or something.

A blue glow that I knew was Satan's magic filled the air.

Satan was safe, thank Hecate!

Then I peered at Sin, who was staring down at me with such open relief and love that it took away my breath. At the same time, the *snarky*, *brave*, and *loving* familiar, who'd helped me break myself free, launched onto my lap, butting me with his head and purring.

"What was that?" Sin's voice was tight.

"You know those traps that I mentioned…?" I replied.

"*It was your worst nightmare.*" Satan trembled, and I stroked him. "*By my whiskers, that was scary. It was meant to separate us, imprisoning us in our own fears.*"

I peeked up at Sin. "What did you see?"

His hands opened and then closed, compulsively. "Fire."

I stroked Satan's head. "And you?"

Satan trembled more violently. "*I was alone. Just…alone. But you're here now.*"

I understood his fear because it was mine as well.

I scattered kisses over his whiskery face.

"*Lay off with the kissing,*" Satan objected, embarrassed. "*Not in front of the shifter.*"

Sin dropped to his knees next to me; his spicy

myrrh scent wove around me. "I don't suppose that we can escape."

I shook my head. "Sorry."

Sin's hot breath gusted against my cheek, and his forehead rested against mine. "On the contrary, I'm sorry that I haven't protected you better. Being separated from you was my true nightmare. The fear that you could be hurt or that I wouldn't be able to save you..." His silver eyes became molten. "In case we die..."

I poked his knee. "Pessimist."

His lips curled into a smile against my lips, which was delicious. "Realist. In case we die, will you allow me one request?"

I narrowed my eyes. "Maybe."

"Kissing sounds wonderful. May I...?"

Yes...yes...yes...

I nodded.

Then Sin's plush lips met mine, and he kissed me.

CHAPTER FOURTEEN

Marchbanks House, Witch Hollow

ASTRA

My magic sparked along my lips, brought to life by Sin's kiss.

In that moment, as I closed my eyes to lose myself in the pleasure, I felt more powerful than ever before.

I thrilled with the warm press of Sin's lips to mine, and the way that his fingers pressed protectively on the hollow of my back.

Sin pressed closer, and his magic stroked over me. I'd never been so possessed, nor so possessive of the man in my arms.

It hadn't been like this with Starlight.

I didn't need a partner to complete me, but it was a delicious bonus.

I moaned, wrapping my hand into Sin's hair. He moaned, as I tugged. He smelled of bonfires and tasted of rich brandy.

When my skin tingled and my stomach lurched, my eyes shot open.

The oubliette groaned and shook. Dust tumbled from the roof, coating us into ghosts. Then I yelped, as the world transformed.

Sin howled, but still gripped onto my arms to stop me from tumbling onto my ass.

He was ever the gentleman.

His magic wrapped around me like wings.

My eyes widened. Wait, they were his *actual* wings. I reached out to stroke them. They were bat-like and a shimmering gray. Sin's ethereal magic fluttered around them like ribbons.

They were gorgeous.

"My wings tend to pop out when I'm excited." A blush spread up Sin's neck. "I never did learn to control myself."

I liked the idea of making him lose control, as long as it didn't involve fire play or other body parts *popping out* when he was excited.

But a kiss…or other sexy times…had never literally made the earth move before.

Wow, Sin was good.

I wasn't letting him go. I cuddled closer into his embrace.

Then Satan darted out from behind me. "*I'm going for a Satan's Personal Achievement Award record. Three-way transportation from inside a warded oubliette is brilliant, right?*"

"You're a genius." Sin smiled, but he looked as dazed, as I felt. That'd been quite a...*life-altering*... kiss. I couldn't pretend that I wanted our relationship to be *fake* any longer. "So, where are we?"

"*Directly above the oubliette.*" Satan held up his paws to me like a toddler asking to be carried (and that was one image that I knew never to tell him unless I wanted to be cursed to always misplace my shoes or worse, my dignity).

I'm not sure that I needed to be cursed for that last one.

I stooped and scooped up Satan onto my palms. I placed him on my shoulder, and he sank his claws in like I was his throne. He tilted up his head, as if he'd been returned to his rightful place.

I guessed that he had.

I glanced around me at the large garden, which prickled with powerful magic. It wove away toward a wood at the bottom. Elven trees towered over beds of roses from every season in a multi-color explosion: whites, pinks, reds, and black. Stone statues like gargoyles stood around the neat lawn, as if a tea party had been hexed by a wicked witch.

I shuddered. *What if it truly had been?*

I wandered to the nearest statue, which was an angel with outspread wings. I caressed my hand along the intricately carved wingtip, and the magic beneath thrummed.

"How'd you get us out?" I asked, weirdly hushed because this garden was freaking me out and not in the happy thrills of a horror movie. This was far more like the living space of a killer, than the inside of the house had been. "And nope, *I'm the Great Satan* is not an acceptable answer."

Satan snapped shut his mouth and then said with a twinkle in his eye, "*Oubliettes are easy. They're where your enemy sends you to be* forgotten. *But the Great Satan is unforgettable.*" Well, that was true. "*So, I just used my magic to reverse the ward's spell and make us* found *again.*"

Was it weird that I was now able to follow Satan's explanations? His discussions on magic made more sense than my tutors' ever had, even though he broke magical rules as often as it appeared the Sheriff broke the law.

I gave the angel statue a final reassuring stroke as if it was one of my familiars and then scanned across to the trees. The spires of Oxford were a dark blur behind the woods.

When I turned to Sin, however, who was leaning against a shifter caught in bear form on his hindlegs, I caught a flash of gold and emerald. Then I saw Piper's pale face peering at us around a stone statue of a fae at the bottom of the lawn.

What was Piper doing here?

He'd told us that Edel wouldn't be at the house for hours yet. So, why would he come to the empty house of his boss?

I froze, glancing at Sin, who shot me a troubled glance. Then his shoulders stiffened like he'd come to a decision, and his expression darkened.

Uh-oh…

"*Watch out, dragon alert.*" Satan snuggled closer to me.

I held out my hand.

Like my hand could do anything against a furious dragon.

Sin's eyes flashed, all predator. He unfolded his wings, preparing to take flight.

How had I forgotten that I'd been cuddling up to (kissing…definitely kissing), a deadly shifter?

But then, I'd always been attracted to dangerous men.

"Hold up," I pleaded. "Let's just talk to the breakable fae, before we go in flames blazing."

Sin snarled, and in a spray of silver glitter, transformed into his full dragon form.

Flames it was then.

Sin was huge and majestic. His silver head and body sparkled in the sunshine; his skin was smooth. He roared and flames shot from his jaws into the sky.

I shivered. *Was it wrong that I was desperate to ride him now in more ways than one?*

When Sin swung his head to look at me through gleaming eyes, I wondered for a moment whether I'd said that out loud.

Then Sin took off into the air, swooping toward Piper. His long neck and tail were sinuous, as he coiled through the cloudy sky. Silver magic fluttered out of his wings like he was wearing a decadent outfit.

"*In the name of worker solidarity,*" Satan hissed, "*can we stop the idiot barbecuing the other idiot, before we get any answers out of him?*"

"More like*: can you?*" I sprinted down the lawn after Sin, dodging between the statues.

"*I could, but this is more fun.*"

"Bad kitty."

"*Always.*"

Piper squealed loudly enough to carry across the garden, before flying into the air himself and diving toward the trees.

He wasn't going to make it…

Flames exploded from Sin like he wasn't able to hold them inside, scorching a path across the lawn, which blackened the grass.

As a scare tactic it worked because the fae dropped out of the sky in a feathery crash landing. He sat up, rubbing his bruised head and then scrambled to his feet.

"Give yourself up," I hollered. "We just have a few questions."

Wasn't that what police officers said?

Of course, usually they hadn't broken into the person's house without a warrant first or turned into fire-breathing dragons.

But we weren't conventional in Evermore.

At my yell, Piper turned to look at me with large eyes like emerald pools. He was terrified but something else too…

Guilty?

I stiffened. I definitely had some questions for the fae.

Piper fell to his knees, holding up his hands in the universal gesture for *I surrender*.

Sin did a victory lap in the air, as his magic wove around him in joyful waves. I allowed him his moment, even if it reminded me of Satan's victory dances.

I wheezed, and my thighs burned, as I ran the rest of the way to Piper, who hunched in on himself, wrapping his quivering wings around himself. He ducked his head, and his emerald hair hung over his face, hiding it.

Sin landed with a *thump*, folding his wings behind him.

"*On my whiskers, that was a fine if scary sight*," Satan said. "*Now turn back, big boy.*"

"For me," I added.

In a spray of glitter, Sin transformed back into a man. "Never call me *big boy*."

I truly was a dragon tamer.

Sin wrapped his arms around his middle. When his gaze met mine, it was vulnerable and open in a way that it hadn't been before.

Had it been a big thing for him to show me his shifer side? *Did he expect me to reject him now?*

I smiled. "You're as gorgeous in your dragon form as you are as a man. I could've done without the extreme fear tactics. Perhaps, we'll work on the flame control."

"You think that I'm gorgeous?" He smirked.

I gave him a flat stare. "That's your take away?"

Sin shrugged. "Always concentrate on the compliment." Then he swept to Piper, gripping his chin to make him look at him. "Now, I don't want to hear any more lies out of your mouth. You know how much I've helped you. We're friends. If that's ever meant anything to you, tell me why you're here."

Piper's eyes gleamed with tears. "I'm sorry."

Sin's expression hardened. "That's not what I asked."

Piper bit his lip. "I wanted to talk to Edel, before you did."

Sin's grip tightened. "You were going to *warn* her?"

"I didn't know what to do, and I needed to ask her permission to..."

Sin dropped Piper's chin and took a step back. "What?"

I cocked my head and studied Piper more closely. He didn't just tremble with fear, the extra element that flushed his cheeks, was *shame*.

He couldn't meet our eyes, bunching his hands in the Magical Blooms apron, which he was still wearing.

Was it guilt, which made him look like that?

"You work at both Magical Blooms and Wild Cupcakes, don't you?" I asked.

Piper nodded, still not looking up. "I enchant their food for them at the bakery."

"Two businesses that Lanira was trying to close." I tilted my head. "Woolsey and his sister seem lovely, and I'd bet that they're your friends. I'd want to protect my friends as well. From what I've seen, everyone looks after each other here in Witch Hollow. Did you and Edel decide to hex her sister together or did Edel put you up to it? We'd understand that as well because she's your boss."

"*This is why we need unions*," Satan muttered.

When Sin caught my eye, I realized the moment that he caught on.

Sin paled, before his lips pinched. "Did you work on the day that Wild Cupcakes catered for the opening at the shelter?"

Piper nodded again.

Sin crouched on one knee next to Piper. "Come on, this is me. I'm not the Mayor or…"

"You were attempting to roast me a minute ago," Piper protested.

Sin shifted, uncomfortably. "Never run from a dragon."

"I'll remember that." Then he held out his hand.

To my surprise, Sin took it but instead of either clasping or cuffing it, he pressed on Piper's wrist. "Your pulse is racing. Look, you know that I'd do anything to save you from the Mayor. But at the moment, you're looking like just the type of suspect he'd love me to drag in to the Council."

"Then arrest me," Piper whispered.

All of a sudden, a blinding white light blasted Sin away from Piper.

I yelped, as Sin crashed into me, and we landed in a tangled pile. Somehow, Satan ended up sitting on top of my stomach, washing his paws.

Satan had a way of landing on his feet.

My head rang, and my vision was blurred. I shook my head and sat up, pushing Satan onto my lap.

Sin groaned, struggling to his knees.

I looked up into the furious gaze of a tall witch with streaming ivory hair, who was dressed in a power suit that instantly made me aware of how stained my own dress was, especially after the grime in the oubliette.

Her hands crackled with white energy. So, that was what she'd hit us with. She stood in front of Piper, protecting him.

Where'd she appeared from? Unless this was…?

"*Edel*," Sin breathed.

Perfect.

The householder was back, we were trespassing, and now we had to face some super charged pissed off all-powerful witch.

Who might still be the murderer.

Sin struggled to stand but fell back onto his ass. Whatever magical shield she'd blasted at us, had sapped our power.

Even more perfect.

Satan wagged his tail in defiance. "*The wicked witch doesn't scare me. I'll defend you.*"

Except, I could sense that his magic had been drained as well. Satan was good at putting up a front.

"It's a spell derived from Dragon Snare," Edel informed us with a calm majesty. "It'll wear off. Plants are more powerful than most witches under-stand." Then she glanced at Piper. "Are you hurt?"

Piper shook his head, shakily pushing himself to his feet. He sheltered behind Edel at her shoulder.

How long would she protect him, when she found out that he could be the killer of her sister?

Unless he was her accomplice.

"Now," Edel said, calmly, "would you mind awfully telling me why you're trespassing in my garden? I'm impressed that you broke my wards but I'm less impressed that you broke in. What would the Founders think?"

Sin stiffened. "Are you threatening me?"

Edel's eyes narrowed. "Were you threatening my employee?"

"Just how did your employee get into Marchbanks House? Isn't he as guilty as us? Are you so keen to hand him over to your shady cabal?" I demanded.

"*Aye, you tell her*," Satan hissed.

"Shady…?" Edel's lips twitched. "He got into my house because the wards recognize that he has *my* permission to enter. He always has. We haven't even been introduced and *you*…" Then her expression softened, as she scrutinized me. *Did I have dirt smeared down my cheek again?* "You look just like her."

"Who?"

"Ursula," Edel answered. "I'm sorry for your loss. She was a wonderful witch. I assume that you're the great-niece who took over her farm. Well, I'd imagine that was amusing, since it's always had a mind of its own. Ursula's garden is the only one in the village that can rival my own, but we were close friends. I admire your endeavor with the familiars. It shows pluck."

Why did I have to like Edel? Nobody had even acknowledged that I was grieving or told me anything about Ursula before.

In all of this, I'd forgotten that Edel was herself grieving.

"I'm sorry for your loss as well," I said, gently.

Edel lowered her hands, and her magic faded. "I find myself not knowing how to feel. It's confusing because I can't believe that my sister's gone. I keep looking around and expecting to see her like a shadow, but she's not there. It's an ache that doesn't go. But I'd be lying if I said that I'm grieving. My sister was a…" She dropped her gaze. "…Well, haven't you been investigating this crime all over the village? Don't you know how she terrorized people, who've already lost so much and are sheltering in Witch Hollow as a sanctuary?"

"You're not convincing me that you didn't murder her." Sin crossed his arms.

"I didn't know that I had to," Edel replied, imperiously.

I glanced at Piper, who'd clasped Edel's hand for support. "Why'd you run toward the trees?"

"I was trying to escape the scary dragon flames," Piper answered.

Yet he squirmed, and I knew that he was hiding something.

Satan's eyes narrowed. "*Cute liar.*"

Piper shot him an apologetic look.

"You were attempting to burn my fae?" Edel demanded.

Sin hunched his shoulders. "Just a little bit."

"I think that he was running to you." I pointed at Edel; I could get a hang of this Holmes thing. "So, why were you sneaking around in the woods?"

"You sound like Ursula too. I could never hide anything from her. She was sharp as a button." Edel leveled me with a hard stare. "What I tell you now is a secret. You must give me your blood oath that you'll keep it."

I glanced at Sin, and he nodded.

"I give my blood oath," Sin and I swore.

Would I regret this?

"For centuries, the Founders have met in a secret ash glade, which is sacred." Edel vibrated with power; it prickled my skin. "The location is hidden from everyone else."

Secret…hidden…meetings in the woods. I bet that they even wore robes.

Yeah, not shady at all.

"If it's so secret, how come Piper knows where you were?" Sin cocked his head.

Edel turned to Piper, gripping him by the arms. Piper shook.

"Can I tell them?" She asked, quietly.

Piper nodded.

"Lord Piper is far more than my assistant at Magical Blooms. He knows my secrets because I trust him. But when he first came to the village, he couldn't control his magic. It slipped out in waves that weren't under his control. The Mayor wished him destroyed."

Piper flinched, and I became pale.

Satan burrowed closer to me, whimpering.

I understood.

Satan had extreme magical power that the Founders could decide was a threat, just like Piper.

In fact, many of my familiars had.

I needed to protect them.

Then I caught Edel's eye, and I understood her. It was what she'd done for Piper, hiding it by employing him so that he hadn't been humiliated.

That didn't sound the actions of a wicked witch but one who was better than most of the witches who I'd met.

No wonder she'd been friends with Ursula.

Sin crawled toward Piper; obviously, his legs still felt like jelly (just like mine did). "I knew that you were clumsy and an accident on wings but…"

"My best friend, ladies and gentlemen." Piper rolled his eyes.

Awkward.

"Best friend?" Sin said.

Piper looked away. "Don't worry, that was just a test. I mean, I have to beat off my friends with a big, *big* stick. You're like just some guy that I know."

"*Uh-huh.*" Sin raised his eyebrow. "Well, some guy that I know, give me a reason to save your feathery behind."

"Please, Sin, I'm sorry. I didn't mean to."

Sin's jaw clenched. "Is that a confession?"

"Just listen to me first, before you haul me away. Edel's been helping me by training me to control my magic."

I had the sudden memory of the Magical Blooms with its deadly plants set up like booby traps.

"Were you training in the backroom?" I asked. "Was it a magical obstacle course?"

Edel glared at Piper. "You weren't meant to try, until I was with you."

Piper hung his head.

"*Grass,*" Satan muttered.

"You know that here in Witch Hollow, we don't press people to share their secrets or their pasts. We settle here because we're either running from something or searching for it. I know that it's private, but we're trying to save both Edel and you from a murder charge." Sin studied Piper. "Plus, where's your scimitar?"

I blinked. "Is this your sword fetish again? Some people would think that you were compensating for something."

Satan snickered.

Instinctively, Sin reached for the hilt of his sword and then dropped it like it was burning hot.

"A fae never willingly takes off his scimitar," Piper explained. "He wears it every day of his life until he dies. It's agony to have it taken from you."

"So, who took it?"

Piper swallowed, shaking his head, unable to answer.

I hadn't realized how much a sword could mean to a fae.

Finally, Piper nodded to Edel, who shot a cascade of light across Sin, Satan, and me like a shower of petal-light rain.

Satan wove his magic around me in a warming blue glow. At the same time, Sin staggered to his feet, stretching out his shoulders. I reached inside myself for the tiny spark of my own magic, which Edel had returned to us.

Edel clasped her hands together. "Lord Piper is an outstanding sorcerer. He was, in fact, the most powerful fae at his Court, which brought jealousy and fear down on his head. The fae admire control over emotion above all else. Lord Piper, as you might have noticed, struggles to control his emotions, as much as his magic." She tapped Piper sharply on the nose. "What they taught you in the Fae Court was wrong. Emotions shouldn't be cruelly suppressed. Their ill treatment of you only worsened your lack of control, rather than helped it." She sighed. "When he embarrassed the Swan Queen…"

"*Now that's a trick that I need to hear about,*" Satan said, gleefully. "*Challenge the system!*"

"Not helping," I muttered.

Edel snorted. "I imagine your familiar is acting out? Ursula's familiar was an absolute terror."

"Lucky?" My brow furrowed. "But all he does is sleep and make vague Emo threats."

Edel grinned in a dark way that made me shiver. "Oh, you just wait. I'd imagine that he's simply warming up to you." That was something to look forward to. Then Edel glanced at Piper, who straightened his shoulders in a show of bravery, which was painful to watch. "Lord Piper was performing magic for the queen when he…accidentally…turned her into a swan."

"*Fae must love irony too.*" Satan chuckled.

"More like deeply unfortunate," Edel snapped. "Lord Piper was severely punished. His scimitar was taken from him and he was locked away. He was only lucky that the fae Prince, Lysander, along with his shifter lover, have more honor than the rest of the

Court. They risked their lives to free him and send him here."

"Bad judge of character that prince if you're admitting to murder," Sin growled, but I heard the hurt in it.

He'd helped Piper and become his friend. And now the pyromaniac fae had killed someone in the village that Sin protected.

I knew about betrayal, and it burned.

"But brave," Piper whispered. "He didn't know that it'd lead to this."

"Wonderful story time," I said. "But what does it all mean? You're admitting…what? You killed Lanira but only accidentally? What even is that?"

"*Manslaughter by magic…?*" Satan ventured. Then his eyes narrowed. "*But even the Great Satan can't produce a Fire Spell by accident.*"

For the first time, Piper spread out his wings in a show of dominance, and magic sparked along them. "Then the Great Satan must not be as a powerful as he thinks." When Edel sent Piper a quailing look, he wrapped his wings around himself again. "*Whoops*, I hurt my case just then, right?"

Sin took a step forward. "Explain. Now."

I shivered. Sin could be scary. Also, hot.

"Not one more step, Sheriff, unless you want to end up on your tight behind again," Edel commanded. *She'd noticed his tight behind…?* Mostly, I hoped that

I was still noticing asses at her age. I *definitely* would be, especially if they looked like Sin's. "Lord Piper is under my protection."

Sin froze. "Even though he burned your sister to a pile of ash?"

Edel winced at the same time as Piper.

"*Accidentally,*" Piper interjected, hurriedly. "That's the crucial word here. Let's not forget it, guys."

"I know what he did." Edel's eyes became milky white with swirling magic, before settling back to crystal blue. "He'll atone. But he had no intent, and magic has a mind of its own."

"*Amen to that.*" Satan grimaced, before correcting himself, "*I mean, damn right.*"

Piper tipped up his chin, defiantly. "This wild magic of mine spills out. I didn't want to say it but I can hear all familiars and thoughts too sometimes. Plus, emotions if they're strong enough. I'm not eavesdropping (much). It just happens."

Satan was never one to back down from a challenge.

He put on his best *thinking hard* expression. "*Not a chance you can read my thoughts, and you can only hear my brilliant self because I'm letting you. Go on then…what am I thinking?*"

Piper blushed. "Are you sure that you want me to tell everybody about something so private? After all, you're thinking about yourself, melted cheese, and—"

"*Aye, he can read thoughts,*" Satan burst out. "*No more proof necessary, cheers.*"

"You don't need to look so smug, Piper." Sin crossed his arms. "Glad as I am that you didn't put me off melted cheese for life, you now get to confess and don't leave out the details."

Piper slowly undid his apron, running his hand over it reverentially, before handing it back to Edel. "I guess that I won't need this again. Thank you, for everything. And believing in me when nobody else did."

"*Don't…*" Edel tried to catch Piper by the shoulders, but he dodged away.

Piper darted to Sin, looking up at him with wide, frightened eyes. Yet he squared his shoulders with a show of courage.

My chest ached.

Was this justice?

I thrilled that Satan and my shelter was safe. We'd discovered the criminal, before the Mayor could hurt Sin in his place.

But was Piper truly guilty?

"I did this, and I won't run away from my punishment again." Piper raised his head to meet Sin's anguished gaze. "The night before the opening of the shelter, I was here in the kitchen of Marchbanks

House. It's where I put the enchantments on the cakes for Wild Cupcakes. Edel can then help me control my magic, if I need it. But then Lanira started this huge row with Edel about Magical Blooms and how she intended to shut it down. I guess that they forgot about me."

"It's true," Edel whispered. "This is all my fault. Piper was my responsibility, and I forgot him to argue with my sister. She always had that effect on me."

"But I couldn't stop my job. It was important to Woolsey that I finished the order in time. I didn't think that it'd be a problem. Only when I heard about how Lanira died…" A tear chased down Piper's pale cheek. "My anger at her must've infused the cakes' enchantments. Many of them included the right ingredients, and Fire Spells need the spirit of Mars. And Mars is the God of War. There was enough of that in the air, since the sisters battled around me. It's why only Lanira was burned. My magic directed it at her alone."

I gaped at him. I'd never heard of a sorcerer, witch, or mage with that level of magic. Now I understood why the Founders had discussed destroying him.

Yet wasn't that as bad as some witches' hatred towards magical familiars? If Satan wasn't tied to me, wouldn't he attempt world domination?

"*Respect*," Satan breathed.

Oh yeah, definite world domination.

"I d-didn't m-mean to. I r-really…" Piper struggled to get out the words through his hitching breath.

Sin pressed his finger to Piper's lips, hushing him. "I believe you. But you never *mean it*, do you? This isn't like getting trapped by a plant, however, or the time that you broke your wings flying face first into the front of the bookstore. A Founder and Inspector is dead. I know that it wasn't intentional, but the Founders will try it as murder."

Witching heavens, I needed to kick some mayoral ass. That was wrong on so many levels.

"No way," I shook my head. "Lanira should be tried as an accomplice in her own murder then because she was part of the spell. It was her arguing that triggered it. I'd say that was…"

"*The Karma Fairy*," Satan crowed.

"And I'm accomplice too," Edel added.

Sin stiffened. "The Mayor would sweep those details aside. Piper is the perfect scapegoat. The Counselors already want to get rid of him."

I brushed the back of my hand against Sin's neck, and his glance at me was long and searching. "How about becoming both a good man *and* a good Sheriff? Because it seems to me that Witch Hollow needs a Sheriff who can stand up to this horrible Mayor and stuffy Founders. Someone who creates his own style of justice."

"You go witch." Piper whooped. When I raised my

eyebrow, he hunched his shoulders. "The criminal waiting on your mercy will be quiet now."

"I'll believe that when I see it," Sin huffed.

"*How about a Sheriff with loopholes?*" Satan wove around Sin's legs. "*On my whiskers, there's always a technicality that can be exploited. So I've heard.*"

Sin crouched down and pulled Satan to cradle in his arms, cuddling him just like I did. "Clever cat."

I winced, waiting for the hiss, scratch of claws, and yelp. Instead, I was shocked at Satan's loud purr.

I thought that Sin wasn't a cat person? And Satan never let other people cradle him like that.

Well, I'd let them have their bromance.

"Loophole it is." Sin tickled under Satan's chin, and Satan shamelessly begged for belly rubs. "Usually, this would be the point that I'd hand the suspect over to the Founders, but you're the closest relative to the deceased."

Surprised, Edel nodded.

Sin took the invitation and rubbed Satan's belly. "I know what it is to lose control of your power and then to have people in authority punish you for it. Lanira's temper caused the spell, along with the natural ingredients in the cake. It's not right that Piper suffer, as if he planned to murder her. There's a statute that declares if a Founder who's a relative agrees to a Sheriff's sentence, then I don't need to take this to the

Mayor. I imagine it was used in more savage times, when relatives wished personal punishments."

"Yey for being civilized," Piper said, weakly.

Edel nodded. "You officially have my permission to sentence Lord Piper yourself."

"I'm taking Piper under house arrest to ensure the village's safety," Sin announced.

Relief flooded through me. When my muscles relaxed, my neck and shoulders ached.

How tense had I been?

The death at my opening had led me to discover my new village, kiss a dragon shifter, and discover friends. But it'd also led me to understanding that there were dangerous authorities at work here, and as much as I wanted to help Sin as Sheriff, I couldn't do that if it made me part of that system.

So, it turned out that I was more of a rebel than I'd known.

"You're mentoring him." I grinned. "I bet he looks up to you and everything."

"I didn't say…"

"You're totally mentoring me," Piper smirked.

"This is no computer games and candy style punishment." Sin's lips thinned. "Silver Hall will be designed, with Edel's help and agreement, to dampen your magic to safe levels. I'll allow her to come over and continue your lessons on control, but until you're safe, you won't leave my house. Luckily for you, it's a mansion. Unluckily for you, you'll be working as my servant to atone."

Satan squirmed in Sin's hold. "*I knew that you were a dragon overlord. Will he be your first slave?*"

Piper's mouth opened and shut. "Your *servant*? Do I have to wear a uniform?"

"You'll have to find out."

Edel shot a blast of stinging magic at Piper's ass, and he yipped. "Show some gratitude. He's just saved you from the Mayor."

Piper grinned. "He knows that I can't quit him. We'll be best buddies and roomies! Of course, I'll also be the one who does the cleaning up after our wild parties, but that's OK because Draco loves me, underneath the seething hatred, which is only a mask, right? Anyway, I'm going to redeem myself, just you wait and see."

Sin groaned, burying his head in Satan's fur. "What have I done?"

Piper laughed and leaped on Sin, covering him in his wings in half hug and half rough housing attack.

I stared down at them, as they rolled on the floor, and Satan jumped on them both in delight.

I'd never seen Satan playing with anyone but familiars before.

He was happy, and I was happy too.

Were we finally safe in Witch Hollow?

Yet what did the kiss with Sin truly mean? And

would both Sin and Piper be in peril now that they'd crossed the Mayor and Founders?

All of a sudden, I was desperate to return to check on Oxford's Magic Kitten Shelter for Familiars, in case the familiars were still in danger.

CHAPTER FIFTEEN

Evermore Farm, Witch Hollow

SATAN

So, now you've ridden the wild adventure, which is the life of a demon familiar.

You're welcome.

If you sacrifice a black kitten plushie on an altar to Hecate on the first full moon of the year, you'll summon a demon kitten of your own.

Go on, try it. It'll only cost you your Soul.

For the love of cheese, did that slip out *again*?

Strokes not Souls…

I need to write a hundred lines of that. Except, I can't hold a pen in my wee paw.

Anyway, Souls or strokes, it'd become known as the Night of the Plushie Slaughter.

Good luck the human cops solving that one.

Yet I, the Great Satan, solved what I like to call The Case of the Exploding B…Witch.

Fair play to them, my witch and the dragon shifter helped. They were my assistants.

In the end, the victim had also been her own killer.

On my whiskers, that took a while to get my furry head around.

Magic was the true guilty party, but so was the Inspector's own petty wars against her sister and neighbors. That was why you should put your faith in the Karma Fairy because she'd find a way to bite you in the ass eventually…*or burn you to ashes*.

The dragon shifter had dragged Piper back to Silver Hall with him. The house arrest appeared as much a punishment for him as it did for the fae. Here's the thing of it, Piper glowed with excitement about becoming roomies with his *best friend*.

Apart from the *servant* part.

I was definitely creating a union.

My witch had rushed back to Evermore Farm like she expected to find it on flames, which wasn't an unreasonable worry considering. Then she'd wandered through the yard, to the stables, and then room to room through the cottage, taking a headcount of every single familiar.

She'd paused to pet each one like she'd thought that she'd never see them again.

To be fair, there were moments in Marchbanks House that even *I'd* thought we'd be trapped forever or killed.

I might've…*just a wee bit*…exaggerated how easy it'd been to break the wards and escape. The ancient magics in Witch Hollow were more powerful than any I'd felt before.

I shivered with excitement at the thought, rolling around in a patch of sweet-smelling daffodils in the yard. Late afternoon golden sunshine warmed me, puddling over the flowers.

Bliss.

The only danger was the chickens, who were pecking around the stables. I was keeping my eye on them. The war wasn't over.

Watch out for my revenge, evil poultry…

I scratched at my ear, lying on my back and soaking in the rays.

I'd already waved my paw over The Secret Diary to fill it with the details of The Case of the Exploding Witch.

You should read it. Kittens are brilliant writers.

I didn't mind playing Dr Watson to my witch's Sherlock, since Watson was the brave retired army type, right?

All of a sudden, Rainbow scampered out of the

cottage and across the yard. When he leaped on my belly, I hissed.

Fluffy bellies were for rubs and not being used as trampolines.

Rainbow shoved his whiskery face close to mine. "*Help me!*"

Instantly alert, I wrapped my paws protectively around Rainbow. "*Who's hunting you?*"

Mice were hunted. It was this whole rodent downside.

Was it the Founders, the Mayor, or pretty much half the village, who we'd crossed on this investigation? My witch had demanded that I increase the protective spells on the shelter, before I take my nap in the sun. She had good reason.

My witch would scold me if I tried to take anywhere over, but it'd be fun to take on the authorities in the village.

She couldn't be cross about that, right?

It'd be fun (and deadly) living in Witch Hollow.

Mysteries, mayhem, and men…

My witch should've known not to tempt fate.

"*No one, see, I was just trying to… I need help with the werewolf,*" Rainbow squeaked.

My tail wagged. "*Woolsey's meant to be in the kitchen on a playdate with you, getting to know you. I knew that I should've chaperoned.*"

Rainbow's nose twitched. "*Carry on you, I'm not a Victorian or choosing a husband.*"

I rolled my eyes. "*Nay, but who you choose to adopt is just as important.*" My witch had made it clear that we *familiars* did the choosing. She was brilliantly unconventional like that. "*Isn't he showing you how to make cupcakes? I told you not to worry; baking's no different to when you do spells with me, apart from the magic and the risk of losing limbs.*"

I brushed at his fur, which was white. I'd never seen him that color before.

What emotion did it mean?

Terrified...?

My own fur bristled. I had some werewolf arse to bite.

But then, the white came off on my paw. Shocked, I licked over the grainy sparkles.

Icing sugar.

Rainbow flushed. "*I fell in the mixing bowl.*"

"*Kittens above, Woolsey was trying to eat you...?*"

Horrified, I rolled over, caging Rainbow like I could protect him from the mouse eating wolf.

Had the adoption all been a ruse to taste exotic demon familiar meat?

I gagged.

Rainbow only giggled. "*I make a fine sugar mouse.*"

I poked out my tongue at him. "*Suck my tail.*"

"*Any time.*"

I narrowed my eyes. "*So, if he wasn't trying to eat you, why'd you come running out of the house screaming: Help me?*"

Rainbow avoided my gaze. "*I'm Ambition Mouse, remember? I don't know what to do because I like him and if I like him, then it means that I need to leave the farm and move in with him and his sister and...I panicked. I'm not saying that I needed a chaperone, mind.*" He held up his paw. "*But I just needed you.*"

"*I love you too, sugar mouse.*" I grinned. "*But it's like this, see, if you like the wolf, then it doesn't mean that it's less scary to make the leap to adopting him. But the life you could have at Wild Cupcakes with a wolf of your own, like I have my witch, could make you shine yellow with happiness more than you can imagine. You won't know until you try. And I won't let you stay there if you're not happy. I'll come and get you, whenever you want.*"

"*And you'll come visit?*" Rainbow asked in a small voice.

"*Try and stop me,*" I assured him.

I meant it: I'd love the challenge.

There were sweet buns with my name all over them.

Rainbow glowed as bright yellow as the daffodils around us. "*Then I have a werewolf to adopt.*"

My magic burst out of me in sparkling joy.

Rainbow was our first success at the Magic Kitten Shelter. I'd insist that my witch took this evening off to celebrate (although, she'd probably choose a long bath and a good book as her treats).

If I could only get my witch to adopt the dragon shifter…

She'd kissed him.

I wrinkled my nose at the memory of the weird kissy faces that they'd made like *they'd* been trying to devour each other.

I didn't want to know about their mating habits, as long as I got to influence…*I meant care for*…their babies.

They'd have such beautiful babies together.

Perhaps, the Karma Fairy would help me in my quest to find love for my lonely witch or would she be doomed to forever sing "Wrecking Ball"?

Because nobody wanted that.

I frowned, before suddenly grinning. I glanced at my witch, who was bustling around the driveway. She hadn't stopped compulsively working since we'd returned like she needed to feel useful to keep us safe.

She *might* collapse in exhaustion again. It was a danger.

I'd better warn Sin, *then he'd better come over*.

The Great Satan was a more skilled matchmaker than Tinder. My witch didn't even have to swipe, and

I'd make her perfect lover appear, clutching a cupcake.

What was more perfect than that?

Would my witch adopt the shifter now?

CHAPTER SIXTEEN

Evermore, Witch Hollow

ASTRA

I leaned on the wonky sign, pushing it back into the earth with a grunt.

Magical words swirled in flashing yellow to match the bobbing daffodils at the entrance to the farm:

Welcome to Oxford's Magic Kitten Shelter for Familiars!

The roots beneath the sign heaved upward in defiance, but this time, I wasn't going to lose the battle against the enchanted garden.

I'd spent the last few days facing far more frightening plants.

"I'm Ursula's great-niece and hey look at that, Evermore's mine now." I jumped up and down; my hair flew out, *thwapping* against my ass. I was spanking myself better than I was spanking the garden. Yet I wove my magic, which felt stronger than it ever had before, deep into Evermore's grounds. "Wave the white flag, and I'll make a deal." *I'd learned that skill from Satan.* "I won't pull out any weeds as hostages, if you leave my sign alone. Agreed?"

All of a sudden, the ground stilled.

Sweat dampened my forehead, and my dress was ripped, where it'd caught on brambles. The antique cat clips hung like they were climbing the drapes on either side of my face.

Then the ground gave a final, grumbling heave, before stilling again.

I sighed, finally righting the sign and then rubbing my hand across my cheek.

And now I had a dirt smeared face as well.

I also, however, had a truce with Evermore. And I'd managed it without Satan diving in to save me.

I hadn't pulled something like that off…*well, ever.*

I glowed with pride. It was okay to pat myself on the witchy back if there was no one else to do it, right?

Yeah, I knew that the gardens hadn't submitted to me. This was just the first negotiation.

Bring it on.

After all, I was the sleuth who'd caught an…accidental…killer…sort of…?

I was claiming it.

Mum hadn't thought that I'd be able to survive outside the House of Demons. I was the witch in the family with the least magic, even if she didn't realize just how *least* I truly was. Gran had encouraged me to get out from underneath mum's wicked shadow, but she didn't understand my drive to protect familiars.

I had a feeling that Ursula would've done.

I smiled, allowing calm to wash over me. Evermore felt more like home now.

The boxes were unpacked, the opening had happened (even if with deadly results), and I'd certainly been introduced to the village with a bang. I'd protected Satan and the other familiars. As long as the Inspectorate approved it, then we were safe.

At least, if I didn't think about those Founders and their clandestine meetings in the woods or the Mayor with his control over Witch Hollow.

For now, I'd rather think about a certain aristocratic dragon shifter, and the way that his mouth had tasted of brandy, while his hand had been warm, stroking my lower back.

Witching heavens, who knew that the boy next door would be as sexy-as-sin?

I snickered at my own joke. Where was Satan, when I needed to pun?

When a flicker of black and white dived across the driveway, I watched the pair of house martins, nesting lovers, swoop to their mud nest that was tucked under the eaves of the converted stables.

This time, I didn't resent their bright *look at how in love we are* chirping.

There was something to be said for PDA.

I glanced back at the yard. Kid lay in the field, playing chess with Frisky. Neither could move the pieces, of course. So, the ferret twins, Pumpkin and Spice, nudged the pieces for them, at each imperious nod of the two large familiars' heads.

I couldn't see who was winning, but from the minotaur's angry snorting, I'd guess that it was the griffin.

Rainbow was in the kitchen with Woolsey. I hadn't wanted to wait on setting up their first meeting, after I knew for certain that the wolf wasn't a killer.

They were a good match, and this would be the shelter's first adoption.

Rainbow deserved to shine yellow, rather than blue. If I could place such a cheeky mouse familiar, then there was hope for all my demons.

All of a sudden, Satan pelted down the driveway towards me. Chickens squawked and flapped, chasing after him.

I rested my hands on my hips.

The chickens *really* didn't like Satan. Perhaps, they had some sort of connected memory to ancient rituals, in which their ancestors had been sacrificed.

I'd better rethink my order that Satan couldn't fight back. On the other hand, they were providing him with useful exercise. Otherwise, he'd laze around in the sun and end up just like Lucky.

I shuddered. I'd never jinx Satan like that again.

"Save me, the chickens are after me. I surrender!" Satan threw himself at me, hiding behind my legs.

I laughed, gently shooing away the chickens. They flapped their wings in victory and strutted back down the driveway.

Perhaps, they should say never work with kittens, demon familiars, *or chickens.*

"Are you okay?" I crouched to pick up Satan, and he nuzzled under my chin like he'd just survived the apocalypse.

I pushed a feather off his head, and he sneezed.

*Ah, cute kitten sneezes...*another thing that I'd never say out loud to Satan, unless I wanted to find my favorite dress scratched or my lipsticks out of order.

I shivered.

"Just give me a moment." Satan panted. *"On my whiskers, that was horrible. I know, why don't we cook a fine roast this weekend?"*

I raised my eyebrow. "A chicken one?"

"*Now you mention it…*"

"How about a lovely vegetable lasagna?" I countered.

"*Traitor*," Satan grumbled but he still licked my cheek.

I grinned. I knew how to cheer him up. I'd spent the few minutes that I'd had spare, knitting something special for Satan. After the awful experience that he'd had over the last few days (he'd never actually been caught out as a chief suspect before), he deserved it.

I fished in the pocket of my dress and pulled out an orange knitted hat. "Ta da!"

Satan froze and stared at the hat.

Look at that, I'd shocked him into silence. *Had that ever happened before?*

I'd been surprised how devastated he'd been to lose his other one at the opening, when it'd become covered in cream. This one was even taller and brighter than the last one to make up for the loss.

I never wanted to see Satan sad. I'd grown up with him as my best friend. I loved him more than I'd ever love anybody, and I needed to show him somehow.

It almost looked like he was about to cry with joy.

I gently settled the woolen hat on his head. It had slits to allow his silky ears to poke through.

He looked adorable.

I gazed at him expectantly.

Satan opened his mouth and then closed it again. It was sweet how he was so overwhelmed at the gift that he could barely get himself to speak.

At last, he blinked at me through his eyes that looked even more emerald in contrast to his orange hat. "*I'll cherish this hat as much as I did the last one. By my tail, I need to go and sulk…I mean sleep…in my nap zone.*" Then he added, "*I want my cuddle monkey.*"

He disappeared with a pop and sparkle of magic.

I stared where he'd been a moment before.

He probably just wanted to show his knitted Hell the knitted hat.

I wouldn't put it past Satan to create a union for all the items that I knitted.

"Your camp for rebel familiars is still standing then?" Sin's aristocratic voice called.

I turned and couldn't help the way that my lips tugged up at the sight of Sin leaning on the fence.

How did I forget how tall he was every time?

He shook his midnight black tumble of hair out of his eyes, and butterflies fluttered in my stomach.

"And your AI mansion hasn't yet been driven mad by the sorcerer fae?" I shot back.

Sin chuckled. "Piper's being infuriating, and Draco and isn't talking to me. Apparently, inviting someone new to live with us without his permission is terrible etiquette."

"So, you're escaping over to your neighbor's?" I asked. "I don't think that you'll discover any more peace or calm here."

"Who said that I was looking for peace or calm?" He shifted with his hands clasped behind his back.

"Your yoga and pilates sessions."

His lips quirked. "Good point. But that's not why I'm here."

Confused, I ran my hand along my flushed cheek and then remembered the dirt, escaping cat clips, and tangled hair.

Oh well, I'd seen Sin screaming, on his ass, and pressed against me in an oubliette.

He'd trusted me enough to show me his dragon form. There was no point me worrying about appearances now. I didn't need to dress up. If he could show both sides of himself to me without shame, then I could do the same.

I tilted my head. "Then why are you?"

Sin leaped over the remains of the broken fence (maybe I'd better get that fixed but then, I didn't want to stop Sin simply popping over from his property to mine). This time, I didn't even attempt to hide my admiration of his athletic legs.

There were definite possibilities there.

His eyes blazed like he could read my thoughts. *Hecate above, please don't let him be able to read them.*

I attempted to school my expression, but his snort told me that it hadn't been successful.

Sin stalked toward me in a way that should've been frightening, but I'd tamed this predator and now, it was simply hot. "I couldn't rest tonight without telling you that I had some strategic discussions with the Mayor about both Piper and you."

"Me?"

"And the shelter. After all that you were put through with the *accidental death* at the opening and Marchbanks' paperwork on the Inspection being burned, then I requested that the Inspectorate fast-track your case." I remembered the file with all the sad face emojis. *Silver linings…* "In fact, I requested strongly that they pass you." His grinned widened. "Congratulations. Your business has now been officially approved."

My eyes widened, before I launched myself at Sin. He let out a startled *oomph*, as I wound my arms around him, resting my head on his chest. I breathed in deeply his rich scent of myrrh.

"Thank you," I murmured.

When I peered up at him, his expression was soft and tender. "You're welcome."

Why was he still standing as if on parade? Was he such an elite that this was how they hugged?

I peered at him. "This hug would work better if you used your arms."

He pinked. "I didn't want to squash this." He brought his hands forward, which were cupped to hold one of the delicious gooey cakes from Wild Cupcakes. The one that I'd loved, when we'd been on the investigation. He'd noticed *and he'd remembered?* "I hear that you've been overworking and are close to exhaustion. I can't have anyone, who I've inherited, doing anything as dramatic as collapsing."

"You went to all that effort for the punchline to a joke?"

Sin blinked at me; his magic fluttered around him in waves.

Wait a minute…

I drew back, and my eyes narrowed. "Satan transported his naughty furry ass to visit you, didn't he? He told you all that nonsense about my desperate need for…?"

Sin looked down at the cake. "I take it that I've been tricked then."

When our gazes met, we burst into laughter.

"I think that Satan wants me to adopt you," I admitted, unable to meet Sin's gaze. "He's always been possessive, and hey, it looks like he's now possessive of you."

"Well, that's high praise from a cat." He stepped closer. "Look at me, Astra." His voice rumbled through me, and I shuddered. *He was so close…* I looked up, meeting his blazing gaze. "I'd have come over with a gift anyway. Satan's intervention was just a good excuse. And I liked the idea of treating you to something that I knew you'd love. It could be the perfect gift to start our courtship."

He pushed his hands against mine, offering the cupcake.

I gasped, slowly taking it. I stared at Sin in dazed silence, as the cupcake melted in my hand.

Official dragon courtship?

I couldn't pretend that this was a fake relationship anymore. Sin wanted to date, right?

I could do that.

"Traditionally," Sin stroked my jaw, "the gift should be something more precious like…"

I kissed him.

Not because we were in danger and about to die, but because I wanted to and it was *my* gift.

Sin's lips were as delicious as I remembered, and the way that he wrapped his arms around my back made me feel safe and loved.

Perhaps, it was worth the risk of trusting him.

"…just like that," Sin murmured, as he pulled away.

Reluctantly, we had to breathe, after all.

Perhaps, Satan could create a Kissing Without Needing to Break for Breathing Spell. Yet was it worth his cackling amusement when I asked for it?

Sin's slow smile against my lips was definitely *precious*. "The gift giving is, of course, only the first step in a long and complicated courtship."

I narrowed my eyes. "When do I back down from a challenge?"

After that kiss, I was adopting this dragon shifter, even if it killed me.

I'd promised no *mysteries, mayhem, or men.* Instead, I'd broken my promise on all three.

I was okay with that.

Yet what adventures would happen next to the demon familiars, Sin, and me in Witch Hollow?

It'd be magically exciting to find out.

The End…For Now

Continue Astra and Satan's adventures in Witch Hollow in A FAMILIAR CURSE NOW
https://rosemaryajohns.com

Thanks for reading **A Familiar Murder**! If you enjoyed reading this book, **please consider leaving a review on Amazon.** Your support is really important to us authors. Plus, I love hearing from my readers!

Thanks, you're awesome!

Rosemary A Johns

X

Sign up to Rosemary A Johns' Rebel Newsletter for FREE novellas. Also, these special perks: promotions, discounts, and news of hot releases before anyone else.

Become a Rebel here today by joining Rosemary's Rebels Group on Facebook!

WHAT TO READ NEXT: A FAMILIAR CURSE!

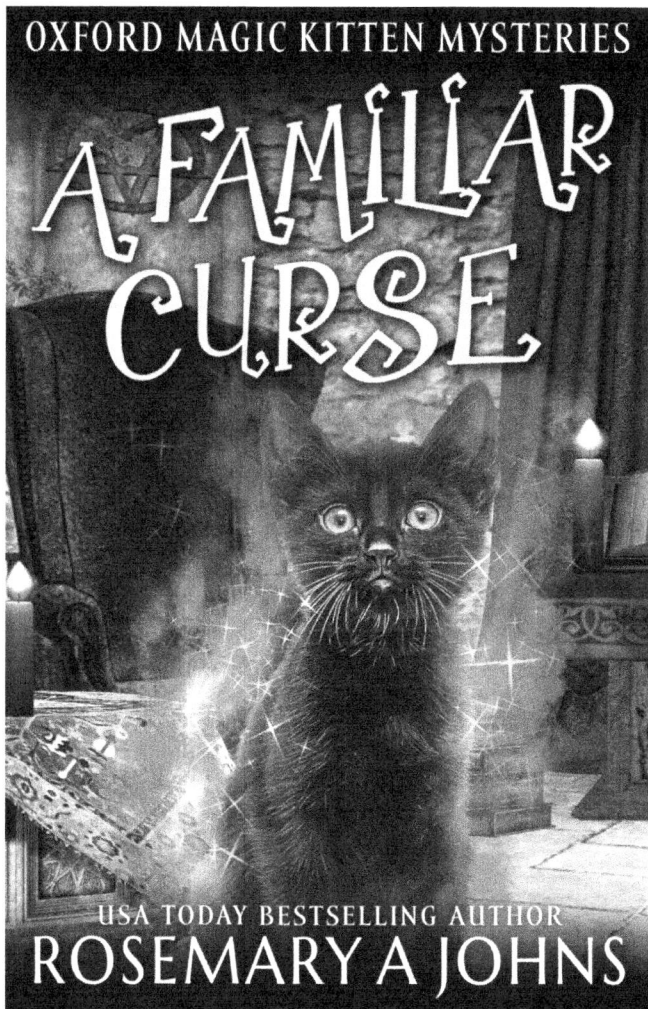

OXFORD MAGIC KITTEN MYSTERIES

A FAMILIAR CURSE

USA TODAY BESTSELLING AUTHOR
ROSEMARY A JOHNS

Welcome to Oxford's Magic Kitten Shelter for Familiars!

My name's Astra, and I'm a witch. This morning, all I want is to take a hot bath without a demon frog familiar insisting that he's a prince in disguise and to read my book without a unicorn nibbling it. Instead, when cursed relics go missing in my picturesque but enchanted village of Witch Hollow, my hot next-door-neighbour, Sheriff, and dragon shifter, Earl Sin, calls on me to become his supernatural Deputy.

Satan, my devilish kitten familiar, knows more than he's telling. But then, what's new?

When a cursed magic flying carpet lands in my attic, its Italian tiger passenger shifts into the handsomest man I've ever seen. All of a sudden, Sin thinks that he's found his suspect, and sparks fly. But I protect familiars, even mysterious strangers with twinkly blue eyes and cheeky smiles.

And all I truly wanted this morning was a hot bath…

One-Click now and decide which familiar you'll adopt today!

A Familiar Curse is Book Two in the Oxford Magic Kitten Mysteries cozy mystery series. Start reading to escape into magic, mystery, and laugh-out loud fun!

READ A FAMILIAR CURSE NOW!

OTHER BOOKS SET IN WITCH
HOLLOW...

Your Invitation To The Magical And Exclusive Oxford Paranormal Book Club!

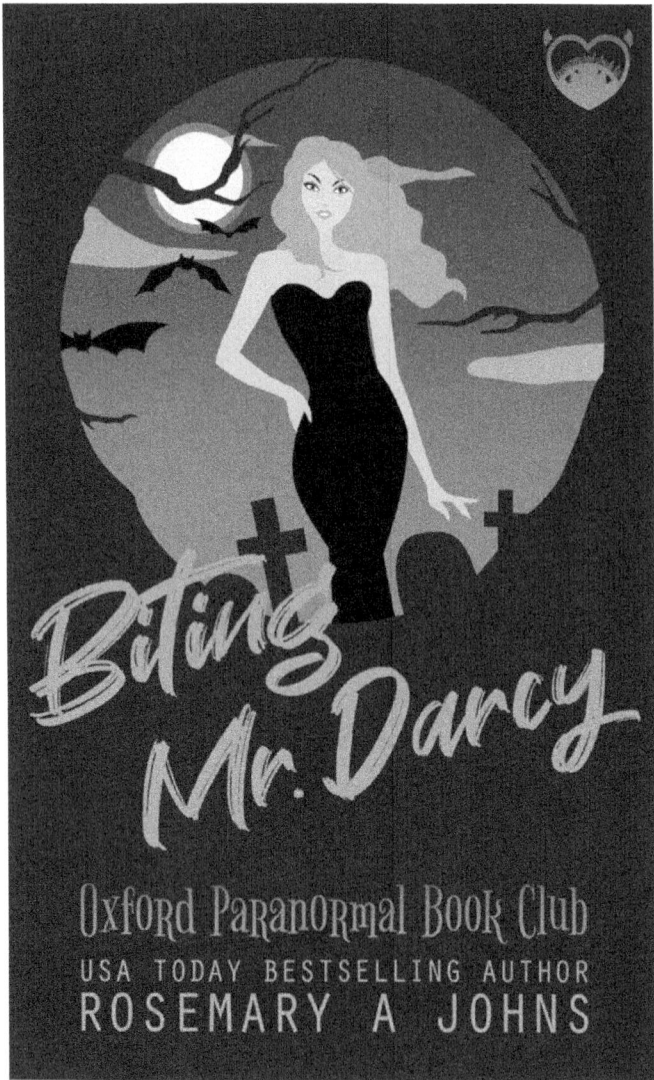

Welcome to Oxford Paranormal Book Club, where your book boyfriend transforms magically to life!

I'm Eva, a sassy vampire librarian whose taste in men sucks. I'd prefer a night in with a Jane Austen novel, rather than a date.

But then the library's Grimoire casts a curse on the book club that I run for witches, werewolves, and dragons in the magical English village of Witch Hollow. Now we can only find our true love from within our Book of the Month. I only realize how screwed I am, when *Pride and Prejudice* jumps open and…

…I'm staring into the smoldering gaze of Mr. Darcy brought to life.

He's aristocratic, arrogant, and convinced that he's real and the rest of the us are make-believe. But he's also wickedly handsome, sexy-as-hell, and with eyes that beg me to bite him. He's maddening, but his touch is maddeningly perfect.

Yet I'm running out of time. Will Darcy be dragged back into *Pride and Prejudice* at the next book club, or can I convince him to become my eternal lover?

Book boyfriends have never felt so real.

One-Click now and join the members of the Oxford Paranormal Book Club for this steamy laugh-out-loud rom-com as Bridget Jones's Diary meets Jane Austen. Get your copy today to take home your own Mr. Darcy!

ABOUT THE AUTHOR

ROSEMARY A JOHNS is a USA Today bestselling and award-winning romance, romantic comedy, and fantasy author, music fanatic, and paranormal anti-hero addict. She writes sexy shifters, fae, and angels, savage vampires, and epic battles.

Winner of the Silver Award in the National Wishing Shelf Book Awards. Finalist in the IAN Book of the Year Awards. Runner-up in the Best Fantasy Book of the Year, Reality Bites Book Awards. Honorable Mention in the Readers' Favorite Book Awards.

Shortlisted in the International Rubery Book Awards.

Rosemary is also a traditionally published short story writer. She studied history at Oxford University and ran her own Oxford theater company. She's always been a rebel…

Thanks for leaving a review. You're awesome!

Want to read more and stay up to date on Rosemary's newest releases? **Sign up for her *VIP* Rebel Newsletter and get FREE novellas!**

Have you read all the series by Rosemary A Johns?
Rebel Academy
Rebel Werewolves
Rebel: House of Fae
Oxford Paranormal Book Club
Rebel Angels
Rebel Gods
Rebel Vampires
Rebel Legends

Read More from Rosemary A Johns
Website
Bookbub
Facebook
Twitter: @RosemaryAJohns
Become a Rebel here today by joining Rosemary's Rebels Group on Facebook!

Printed in Great Britain
by Amazon